MW01075900

HARMATTAN
SEASON

HARMATTAN
SEASON

a novel

TOCHI
ONYEBUCHI

TOR

TOR PUBLISHING GROUP
NEW YORK

HARMATTAN SEASON

Copyright © 2025 by Tochi Onyebuchi

A Tor Book
Published by Tom Doherty Associates / Tor Publishing Group
120 Broadway
New York, NY 10271

www.torpublishinggroup.com

Tor® is a registered trademark of Macmillan Publishing Group, LLC.

Library of Congress Cataloging-in-Publication Data

Names: Onyebuchi, Tochi, author.
Title: Harmattan season : a novel / Tochi Onyebuchi.
Description: First edition. | New York : Tor, a Tom Doherty Associates
  book, 2025.
Identifiers: LCCN 2024059286 | ISBN 9781250782977 (hardcover) |
  ISBN 9781250782984 (ebook)
Subjects: LCGFT: Thrillers (Fiction) | Detective and mystery fiction. |
  Novels.
Classification: LCC PS3615.N93 H37 2025 | DDC 813/.6—
  dc23/eng/20241213
LC record available at https://lccn.loc.gov/2024059286

Our books may be purchased in bulk for promotional, educational, or business
use. Please contact your local bookseller or the Macmillan Corporate and
Premium Sales Department at 1-800-221-7945, extension 5442, or by email
at MacmillanSpecialMarkets@macmillan.com.

First Edition: 2025

Printed in the United States of America

0 9 8 7 6 5 4 3 2 1

To C.

HARMATTAN
SEASON

CHAPTER ONE

Fortune always left whatever room I walked into, which is why I don't leave my place much these days. It works pretty well; I keep my office close (downstairs, actually) for others' sake. Means that the bad-luck radius stays small. But, of course, the work suffers. The neighbors under my office too noisy with all their kids and uncles and grandparents—three whole generations of ruckus in maybe four rooms tops—and never enough jobs to keep the tax collectors off my back. But, hey, they show up and knock on my door, they'll stub their toe on the way in. Maybe bang their head against a loose piece of doorframe or get into a fight with their wife later that night. Not my fault, right? I did my best. But if the interest on my late school fees is worth it, who am I to stop a man?

Still, I got a nice east-facing window so when the sun comes through in the mornings, it wakes me out of my shisha stupor. When I'm not already up because a sleepless night is the bequest of a guy like me.

All of which is to say I like my life. Rather, I'm good with it. I don't need much. I certainly don't need trouble. But that's the thing about living in a town, living with other people. Need finds you.

And I guess you can say it's need that's banging on my door in the middle of the night.

The neighbors are loud enough that I don't hear it at first. Just another peal of thunder in the storm. But then the thuds get sharper. They get that particular wood-threatening crack to them. People don't knock like that. Trouble does.

My eyes open, I stare at the ceiling for a few wishful moments, then I lower myself to the ground. Sometimes, Floating helps with the sleep. Sometimes, it just makes everything worse. I should've known not to open the door. But maybe a part of me hopes that whoever's on the other side is gonna see the rug on the floor, the bare mud-and-brick walls, the closet with a rolled-up prayer mat and too few clothes in it, my rusted bathing pot, and think to themselves "You know what? Let me give this guy a break. He could use it."

Who am I kidding?

The lock's barely undone before the body tumbles through.

I don't try to catch the crime scene dragging itself across my floor. Instead, I just try to close the door as quietly as I can. She's holding her stomach when she brings herself up against my far wall. My window wall. No, Mister Ofisiden Ye, I don't know what this profusely bleeding woman is doing in my apartment, I figured the neighbors downstairs would've stopped her.

At least this one's gracious enough not to make too much of a mess.

"You . . ." she tries to say.

A person who isn't me would likely try to pry her hand loose from her stomach, get a good look at what's got her sweating every ounce of water in her body. Instead, I'm me, so I just stand in the middle of my bedroom and wait for this whole thing to explain itself. But she just looks up at me. Gets a good look at my face and stops trying to make words. And we're like that for a time—me standing, her letting out shuddering breath after shuddering breath—caught in a painting. Then there's something downstairs that actually worries me. The neighbors are quiet.

"Hide me. Please."

Where? I wanna ask her. I sleep and shit in the same room. But there's a thing in her eyes that does it for me. Always the eyes. Even through the strands of long black hair pasted over her forehead, hair glowing silver in the moonlight, I can see those eyes.

So I help the poor shivering girl to her feet and shuffle her to the closet. There's less than enough space for her, even if she folded herself in two. But I make it work the best way I can.

Footsteps. Right before my unlocked door swings open, I nudge my water pot over the bloodstain she left on the floor right under my window.

Two ofisiden ye fill the doorway, all spears and cinched robes and red turbans, and I'm supposed to be nervous. What does it for me is seeing the tip of someone's tarboush behind them.

"Moussa," I say to the policier in black who steps between the two ofisiden ye.

He sighs like he's disappointed in seeing me, like I chose to be wrapped up in whatever's his business. Like he didn't already know I live here. Or maybe that's why he's sighing. You really live like this? in the form of a sigh.

"Bouba," the policier says to me.

"I usually get tea leaves from the family downstairs; otherwise, I'd offer you tea—"

"Outside." He turns his back. That's my signal to go.

I spare one last look for the two ofisiden ye, then squeeze past. A little too roughly. It's in Allah's hands now. "No chance I can get my sandals, eh?"

"Now."

I'm not the only one barefoot on the chilly dirt road outside the building. The family's huddled by itself, but there are other clusters. Onlookers, maybe work buddies. Maybe a few people caught up in adultery. Not my business.

I can't keep from turning my eyes to where I know my apartment sits. Those goons are probably turning the place over right now. Maybe they're wishing there was more to turn over. But they're gonna find that bloodstain, and I bet they're not even gonna ask me a single question before I get a hand under each armpit, a cane to the back of my knees, and a trip to the kaso.

Instead, I catch Moussa descending the stairs. No ofisiden ye behind him. The crowd disperses from the building entrance. He doesn't seem to notice. Lights up a français, lets the acrid smoke spread the townsfolk farther afield. He knows they can't stand the stuff. It forms a shield around him. He's got power—he's a policier—but he's too disgusting to get near. I can relate. To the being-disgusting part, at least.

The residents see he's heading my way, and I catch a little of that look, that "they are alike" look. But they don't get it. Moussa's a cop. I'm a chercher. The people I find generally don't go to jail. Doesn't mean they don't deserve to.

Moussa winds up standing next to me. He doesn't meet my eye.

"How do you gain weight when you barely eat?" he asks me.

"I should ask you the same, all those français you smoke. Your belly's bigger than mine."

"Where is she?"

"Don't know what you mean." When I should've said "where's who."

"Her trail leads straight here and up those stairs."

"Don't know what you mean."

There's stirring behind us. I'm sure this means the ofisiden ye are officially out of the building. I'm not latched to a crossbar yet.

Maybe my bad luck's run out. "You sure this is how you wanna do this?"

The moon's a special kind of bright tonight. You wouldn't know it's Harmattan season. No trace of a dust haze. The dry in the air is the kind kind. Not the evil kind. Not the nosebleed kind. It's good weather for the type of person who has trouble sleeping.

"Boubacar?" Moussa says. Knocks me out of my enjoying myself for a minute. Sounds like I'm not Bouba anymore.

"Yeah?"

"I'm gonna have to take you to the station, aren't I."

Never wanted one of Moussa's smokes the way I do now. But I got enough français in me to gray both my lungs ten times over. "At least let me get my sandals."

"Ain't that far a walk."

"Moussa."

A sigh, this time from Moussa. "Fine. You got a minute."

I take my time heading back up the stairs. And I make sure Moussa sees it.

Back in my living room–bedroom–sometimes cleaning room, I head to the window wall. Water pot's still there. The moonbeam shoots past it. And of course I have to see what's under it. Blood-stain's in shadow. Still there, but in darkness. You wouldn't see it if you weren't looking for it.

"Hmph."

Now it's the closet's turn.

Nothing.

I don't know why I expected any different. Not because of the way the ofisiden ye left the apartment complex. And not because of the way Moussa elected not to make a show of arresting me. But because, in a case like this, strangeness is the worst kind of luck.

I pick out my sandals and slip them on, then slap-slap my way back downstairs.

I halfway have my arms out to be bound, but Moussa's nowhere to be found. The ofisiden ye are just as vanished. Spectators and gawkers still crowd the street. But the folks who are supposed to haul me in for questioning are gone.

Back upstairs, I kick off my sandals and lie on my rug.

No luck trying to sleep, no matter how little I care about what happened to that girl.

CHAPTER TWO

It's nothing but a pile of small scrolls at the bottom of my door when I come down to my office. Daytime announces itself outside. Natural light covers the staircase, though I still don't know what window it shines through. And everyone's off to work or school. So, aside from some birdsong and the very far-off pinking and thudding of construction, I finally have my blessèd quiet.

I hate it.

Well, "hate"'s a bit strong of a word. I haven't hated anything for a very long time. Strong dislike, sure. Very strong dislike, absolutely. But hate's the type of thing to get a person to wanna erase a thing from the face of the land. Hate's a burn-your-crops-and-salt-your-land kinda thing. Last thing I felt that way about was maybe mosquitoes. But that wet season was worse than most.

Some would say they hate the French that they're seeing more and more of these days. Maybe they hate that their language is mandated in schools now. Maybe they hate that their kids have picked up some of the slang. Maybe that hate comes from those folks worrying French will nudge out their own language and in a generation or two, they won't even be an afterthought. Just some fading memory. Footprints in the desert covered up by a passing sandstorm. I bet they hate the new clothes that cost half a harvest to get. The boots you have to constantly shine, the pantalon, all of those unnecessary bits and pieces to hang on your body when a simple djellaba will do. That's how you know they must've come from somewhere cold. Why would I paste three layers of clothing onto my skin during the wet season? But that's not hate. That's more annoyance than anything else. It's something to laugh at if you're the laughing type.

You don't hear a lot about the folks who violently hate the French. War's deep enough in the background that anybody alive now has probably only walked past it. It's the bullet grazing your cheek. Or the loud banging of a neighbor upstairs. It's a couple hundred paces down the main drag or around a corner and out of sight. Anybody who had a loved one killed by the French has done a pretty good job keeping their mouth shut about it.

I'll tell you what I hate. Loans. The French took our juru system and turned it into this chimera of crédit and débit, and they said "that's how we're going to fund your education," and of course we all said yes and now I owe more in loan payments than I've ever seen cumulatively in my life up till now. Because we told them interest was illegal, and they pointed a gun at us and said "shut up."

In the beginning, though, the French were really good for work. The thing that happens whenever there's suddenly more people around is that it's much easier to do a crime. The thinking behind that? It's much easier to get away with it. Villages don't do anonymity very well. Cities, though? Go to sleep, then wake up to find that someone's fire-painted a chieftain's face on your wall or the fleur-de-lis. A moment's inattention and your money-pouch is gone. Damn the French for introducing the very concept of a money-pouch. It was a lot more difficult to snatch a full-grown goat off someone's shoulder. Still, there wasn't much of a missing-persons industry before the French came along. More crime means more people go missing. Sometimes a young Frenchman falls in love with a dugulen girl and, against the wishes of both families, they abscond. Kids don't get far usually, especially if they're hampered by a Frenchman who doesn't really know the lay of the land, doesn't know his berries, his animal calls, how to mask his tracks. Sometimes, a dugulen goes missing and I eventually run up against the wall of French bureaucracy or, occasionally, French malfeasance. Ain't too hard a lock to pick. But it means finding out that some French official's secretly a serial defiler and murderer and there's a shallow grave somewhere on the city outskirts. Or it means following some missing child's trail to a French household where some wealthy patron's dressed them up like a doll and changed their name. And there ain't a damn thing you can do except tell the parents their kid is French now. Don't bother making a new one, because you don't know who's gonna try to steal that one too.

I get calls from the French sometimes. They're a lot stingier. The more official their title, the less they pay. And I get it. They have policier. And they've started recruiting among the locals. But I'm what folks call a deux-fois and I've been around, so there's just stuff I can do that their officers can't. So when a French person goes missing, I'm the one that's gotta find the disaffected wife who has decided to take up with her dugulen lover. I'm the one that's gotta track her to some village past the outskirts of the arrondissements or even past that and convince her that, hey, if she doesn't go back, her army husband's gonna start shooting the locals. Or, worse, conscripting them. But sometimes some French teenager leaves. And sometimes I have to tell the parent or parents where I found their kid. Doesn't make me happy to watch them learn that sometimes there aren't any happy endings. I'd have to hate a person to want that for them. But that's the job.

Until lately.

No new cases for months now. Nothing. Just bills.

I've got the scrolls on my desk now. I catch myself shaking my head. This whole talking-to-myself thing's gotta stop. Not like I got all the company in the world.

I can't talk to any of my old partners about this. They don't get it. They wouldn't get it. They'd get all sentimental about the thrill of the chase. Like they were hunters the way their ancestors were hunters, all skirts and loincloths on the savannah. Or they'd talk about how this was them doing their duty by their people. The world is changing, and they are the straight lines organizing the chaos of progress. Protecting the dugu. Who's gonna tell them that the dugu is long gone? That there are too many people now. Soon as there's a word for "stranger" in your language, then you've lost that. Now all that's left is the money. That's what I do this for. Money. Not 'cause I want it, but because, if I want any peace in my life, I need it.

That's what all these scrolls on my desk are now. Bills. Another moon of nonpayment on the interest (which is, again, illegal under my religion), and I'm gonna lose the office. Another nonpayment after that, then that ghul of a lender swallows up my bedroom too and all zero pieces of furniture in it. There's always something for them to take. You could tell yourself you don't have a centime or coral to your name, and that percepteur would find something. There's always something.

I've only got so many thoughts and worries and anxieties to go through before I got a picture of that bloodstain on my mind again. It was still there when I went back last night. Under the water pot. No trace of her in the closet, not even a speck of red. Like I'd dreamed up the whole thing. Which would be in keeping with the kinds of dreams I've been known to have.

But I know that's not the end of it. Feels like I got off too easy.

My work runs perpendicular to policier work. When we

cross paths, we're usually heading in different directions. I'm getting in their way or they're getting in mine. A crime happens and if there's a trace of me along the way, they sometimes just go ahead and name me an Involved Person just to get me to back off. Rarely works, but I'm still surprised last night's dialogue was as short as it was. No warning, no hint of things to come. No threat. I didn't even get a good look at her face. Just those eyes.

Well, whatever help she needed was beyond me to give.

Maybe they just lost her trail. Maybe they were fishing, got a tip that she was somewhere in the neighborhood. If I'd stayed out a little longer, maybe I would've caught them making the rounds, doing to everyone in the arrondissement what they'd done to me and the family downstairs. Might've seen the sideways glances the locals gave to the French policiers and their dugulenw foot soldiers. Not my problem anymore. I make a mental note to get some water from the family downstairs and go about cleaning that bloodstain upstairs. Pretty sure it's not evidence of a crime, but it never hurts just to be sure. I think. This would be one of those cases of me getting in their way again, I guess. My work being perpendicular to theirs. Except I got no work.

Maybe if I move these scrolls from one side of the desk to the other, they'll magically disappear. Maybe they'll turn into coin or coral. Maybe the percepteurs'll forget about me. Just another hopeless case of lost tax revenue. Anonymity would be nice.

There's a knock at the door.

"My rates are on the side wall," I call out to the prospective customer. "Half payment upon accepting the job, the other half on delivery of the bad news."

But standing in the doorway isn't a prospective customer. In fact, I'd say he's pretty much the opposite of a prospective customer.

"Peace be upon you, Detective."

"You're wanted at the station, Bouba."

"Sure, Moussa," I say, pushing up from the desk. "Of course I'm wanted at the station."

They never forget about you when you want them to.

CHAPTER THREE

You can tell it's still daytime by the light coming through the hole above my head. Moussa has his back to the door. He's leaning against it, in fact. And he's got his arms crossed. Meanwhile, I'm sitting on a ground mat convinced I'm supposed to have rope around my wrists.

"No, this isn't a social call," Moussa tells me in response to my question.

"Money tight? That why you ain't take me out for kafe?"

"Come on, Bouba. Give me something."

I pull out my pockets. Then I shrug.

"You weren't like this in the sorodassi."

"Maybe I'm like this because of the sorodassi."

Which gets me a frown from him. "This Trickster God riddle shit the reason why you're out of work?"

"Next job's right around the corner."

He sucks his teeth. "Okay, enough of this. Where is she? And don't say you don't know what I'm talking about."

"I don't—"

"Came through the Twentieth last night, raising all kinds of ruckus. Banging on people's doors the whole night. Waking families up while they were sleeping. Woke up the whole damn neighborhood. We tracked her to your place."

"We? You speak French now?"

"We both do. Describe her for me."

Her face flashes before my eyes. The hair pasted to her forehead. The sweat sheening her cheeks. The wide fear and clearwater clarity in her eyes. Like she knew exactly where she was while she bled out on my floor. "Who was she?"

"That shouldn't really matter to you." A beat. "Just whether you seen her or not."

"C'mon."

"You fishin' for a case here? No one to pay you."

"She sure sounds like missing persons."

"She's a terrorist."

I'm waiting for Moussa to say more. He just lets the sentence sit in the dust cloud it raised. A piece of meat on the floor between us for me to gobble up. He wants to see how I react. "Then why aren't the Red-and-Blacks involved? Why they still got you tracking her down?"

"Because this ain't their business either."

"Much rather put a lid on this before it gets bigger than it should."

"That's the office line all right."

"She dugulen?"

Moussa doesn't answer. Which is answer enough.

"This type of thing never used to happen. Used to be, you were hurt or you died, the village knew. It was the village's business. And there was always someone to take care of you, help you along to wherever you were headed, no matter who you'd crossed." I don't know why I said all that. Maybe it has something to do with that girl's eyes. "If she's dugu, maybe check the Temple?"

There's a new softness in Moussa's posture. Like he's sad I gave something up. Or grateful. "We did. No new admits. No one fitting her description."

"So what're you asking me for?"

"Maybe she said something to you. Gave you something to hold for her?"

"Something she could come back for? She a part of something bigger?"

"They don't pay me enough to know that. I just have to find her, that's all."

"Maybe she got in a knife fight. Maybe her husband hit her. Doesn't have to be anything bigger than that." Why am I talking like this? Maybe a part of me wants the question of the girl to have a simple answer. Something small and straightforward. Girl runs from abusive husband. Girl gets robbed. Girl gets attacked by a lion while picking vegetables. Short, simple sentences. No question marks. No mystery. We never had a word for "terrorist" before the French came.

"Maybe." Moussa uncrosses his arms, slides down the door so we're sitting at eye level. "The French say they're bringing order, but it's nothing but chaos since this place has grown. That's what it feels like. All their straight lines just give people something to run outside of. It's not cages and control, we're not animals. But . . . I don't know."

"You miss it too."

"We broke that."

"Yeah." I look at the floor. "We did."

"Look. I gotta wrap this up soon. Government wants police details manning the election spots for the vote, and that means taking my guys off the street. Means there's no one scaring away the diarow and fagakilelaw."

"Thieves and killers vote too."

"Hmmph."

"You think . . . you think she's connected to . . . never mind. Above your pay grade."

"The Commission?"

"Yeah. You always could finish my sentences. Even in the sorodassi."

Moussa shakes his head. But that doesn't mean "no." "This Truth and Reconciliation Commission wahala, it's nothing."

"If it was nothing, your shoulders wouldn't be tense enough to hold up a library." I lean back. "And, hey, jail ain't so bad. You should try it sometime. They even let your old army buddies visit and interrogate you."

"That's not funny, Bouba." Then he holds my gaze. "Lot of men get left behind they keep looking over their shoulder."

I want to say something cheeky about how Moussa's whole job is about looking backward. How it's all about past tense. Figuring out who did what to whom. Where they did it. When and how. Always "did." And never "do." But then, if he hasn't snapped out of this existential poet mode, he'd say something back about how his job working for the French is all about prevention. Future tense. Stopping the "will do" from happening. Looking fierce enough on the streets or imposing enough in their uniforms or with those stripes on their sleeves that "did" never happens. Maybe I'm projecting. My whole job is retracing steps, learning what people's habits and haunts were, their relationships, their history, their desires, their fears. Using those things to figure out where they went to. Fill in the void they made with their absence.

The sun has shifted. Moussa's half cast in shadow.

"You're not making it up, you know."

"What?" Breaks my heart to pull Moussa out of this new reflexive posture of his, but it breaks my heart just as much seeing him sad like this.

"When your kids or grandkids ask about how it was like or when they try to imagine it for themselves and you tell them, it might sometimes feel like you're making it up. Like you're describing some place that never could've existed. But the world gets flatter and who knows where they'll end up and when they ask about what this place was before the French and you tell them, you won't be making it up. Even though that's what it might feel like."

"You know what my kids are thinking? Get them to listen to me and stop staying out so late."

It's good that we're chuckling again. This is the old Moussa. This is also the sloppy Moussa. The Moussa who's more likely to let info about the wounded girl slip.

"Doesn't inspire a lot of hope knowing I'm gonna turn into a lazy assumption. Get old enough and you just turn into something they run away from. Get even older and turn into something they long for."

"That's how it is with us weak-feet." A sigh from me. "At least they still have us policing our own."

"For now."

I can feel my eyebrow rise.

Moussa catches my look. "There are always new français coming. Moving in. Mostly young folk. Newly married or about to be. But it's only a matter of time before it's all diéman on one side of town and us on the other. Color line's inevitable. The way it is now, we at least get to keep a little of the old ways."

"The old ways . . ."

"That's why I gotta find this girl. Before the Commission. Before the election. Before more français get involved."

There it is. "'More'?"

"Let's just say I'm not eager to give the diéman an excuse for putting more straight lines in our lives."

"Maybe that's what she was after too." I tense up at the thing I'm about to say out loud. "You think a Frenchman did to her what was done to her?" A beat. "You think a Frenchman mighta hurt her?"

"I don't know what to think."

"You're still thinking, though." I push myself to my feet. Feels a little premature. Moussa hasn't said I can leave yet, and he might look at me standing over him, casting shadow over him, as some sort of power play, but it's anything but. "I can help."

"No."

"There are questions you can't ask. Questions they don't pay you enough to ask. Well, guess what. Nobody's paying me for anything. Means I can ask whatever questions I want."

He doesn't get up. "For your own good, Boubacar. Drop it."

"You know you're the only one I'd let lock me up."

"Don't be cute. I'm serious." He still hasn't gotten up. He must really be tired. "This has to stay a family affair. Otherwise, no one's safe."

"Safe like that girl was safe."

And that earns me twin daggers where Moussa's eyes would be. "I'm serious."

I watch him get up. He pushes the wooden door open and stands in the doorway almost like he needs to make sure I actually do what he says. Leave and leave it alone.

Maybe he's hoping the lack of payday'll be enough to scare me away.

Maybe he doesn't realize just how bored I've been.

Maybe I'm not giving him enough credit. He did warn me about what I was set on getting into.

CHAPTER FOUR

Someone on the outside looking in might look at me walking through the Twentieth and working my way closer and closer to the city center, taking the long way, heading to where I'm heading, and think I'm shirking my duties. They might think I'm worried about following the trail I started sniffing during my interrogation. The trail that started with that bloodstain on my floor. Me being inscrutable to myself, I might think that too. So I might ask myself why I'm now standing in front of this ugly stone building with no sign out front. And I might ask myself why I tell the front desk I'm here to see Oumar Coulibaly. Why, when the receptionist tells me he's not expecting anyone, I tell her the truth, that I'm an old friend. Why I smile when I say it.

But then I sit at the round table with that old, graying man with his belly like a ballon's been taped to his stomach, and I know the real of it all. This is my work.

"Hey, Oumar."

"Peace be upon you, as well, Bouba." His voice is gravel. His gaze is cast out the window. His mind is a thousand miles away.

"They're obviously feeding you well here."

"All my life, I've been well fed." No change in intonation or voice, just that same slow, scraping sound.

Plain French women in plain French dresses and aprons walk by. Some carry trays with steaming teapots and glasses. Some carry tinctures and droppers arrayed neatly next to the little tins. The ones that aren't silent whisper kindly to their charges. Men just like Oumar. The ones with the scars on their faces and the burn marks on their bodies. The ones with the limps. The ones who stare off into the distance.

I know one of Oumar's eyes is glass, but it's the one I can't see. Maybe he's being polite for this visit. He hasn't had time to cover it, didn't know I was coming, so he's sparing me or something.

A nurse lays a metal tray on the table between me and Oumar. She smiles at me without revealing any teeth. I thank her and set to pouring. Then I place Oumar's glass close enough he won't have to reach to get it. Just a brief re-angling of the wrist and it's his.

"You know, I saw Moussa today." No reaction from Oumar. "He's doing well. Eating well. Um, he's a little lost, though. I think he should retire. Didn't tell him, but I think he could smell it off me. Or maybe that was something else. Has he been to visit? Moussa?"

"Why would Moussa come visit me?"

"I—It's . . . you were his friend too."

Oumar doesn't even glance at his glass.

I look around me at this place with its open space and its high ceiling and the stone windows and it feels cold. Feels chillier than any place in this land. Like all the cold night air that's ever existed comes here to find a home. It feels so foreign to the rest of our home with its open spaces and its sun and its fierce winds and even how the rain is warm when it comes. And I wonder how the French do it. How they manage to bring cold with them everywhere they go. I sip my tea.

"Anybody been by? The kids? The missus?"

Was that a flicker of something on Oumar's face? His home life's a black hole. A complete and utter mystery. But I do know he was loved once. Even after the war. This place is filled with

men who were loved. By somebody. I can only hope that there
was a mother or sister or woman somewhere who felt some type
of way about them. Who could carve through the ice of a man.
But there I go again, thinking I'm terminally unique. We were
all in the sorodassi. Maybe the only difference between them
and me is I never got wounded enough that it took the light out
of my eyes. I been shot at, been shot. I been cut through. There
were times it looked like I would lose an arm or a leg or an eye,
but Allah saw me fit for something else. We were all of us in the
war. Long time ago, I stopped asking myself why I made it out
when all these men around me didn't. When it turned out that
Oumar didn't. So I should stop asking myself when Oumar's finally gonna pick up that damned cup of tea.

"Look. A girl came to see me."

Oumar's real eye flicks at me, then away. He knows something.

"She was in a bad way. Didn't say what she wanted from me.
Didn't seem like there was anything I had to give her. But . . ."
Time to gamble. "But it got me thinking that maybe the war's not
over. For some people."

"You gonna say some crap about justice again?"

"No, I—"

"'Cause it's bullshit. Ain't no such thing." Now, he turns to
face me, and I see the glass eye, and maybe he was being polite,
because the thing now scares the shit out of me. "Me sitting here
is justice."

"I'm not here to talk about that."

He calms. Like a fire that had been burning around him has
gone out.

"I know you don't go for that kinda thing."

"Maybe Moussa's feeling introspective now and thinking
about the past or whatever, but what's happened has happened.

And whatever's waiting for us after, well, justice is fake, but 'deserving' is something else. What a man deserves is real."

"And what a man doesn't deserve?"

"You're not safe either."

And now I want to punch him in the face. "This isn't about me. I'm just talking."

He takes his glass, brings it to his lips, and takes the tiniest sip of tea I've ever seen in my life. "You didn't put in any sugar."

"Your teeth don't need it."

"I'll tell you what my teeth do or don't need."

There's still half a glassful of tea left but I refill my cup.

"This Commission's a good thing."

I pause mid-refill.

"You ask me, it's what we all deserve."

I finish pouring and set the pot down gently. "What are you talking about?"

"It's a way to set things right. Balance accounts. Pay our blood debt. Guilt got nothing to do with it. You feel how you feel, that don't change what you did. Ain't enough to whisper you're sorry or to go about your life thinking you'll never do it again. 'Cause the time may come when you're called on to do it again, and who's to say you've changed?" He doesn't sound like he's trying to convince himself.

"And the jatigewalekela?"

Now it's Oumar's turn to look hurt.

"What about their blood debt?"

"Don't get angry on my behalf, Bouba."

"I ain't angry on your behalf, Oumar. I'm just chasing something, someone, who might be mixed up in a thing too big for her."

And for some reason, Oumar looks the softest he's ever looked around me. Maybe he feels protective of this imaginary person.

That father instinct kicking in. Maybe it's part of his whole moving-on thing. Or maybe it's something I can only guess at. But he's holding his glass now like it's something he wants to take care of. He's got one hand underneath the base and the other hand wrapped gently around its sides. "How would I know anything about that?"

"Oumar, jatigewalekela put you here."

"We don't know that's what happened to my home."

"Don't be stupid. Your house didn't blow up by accident."

He almost flinches at the mention, and I almost feel bad for bringing it up.

I lower my voice to a hiss. "This is what I'm talking about. With the war not being over for some people." I move in closer. "Moussa's already after her. I'm thinking, if I can get to her first, then maybe . . . I don't know."

"Maybe what?"

"I can . . ." But I don't know what else there is to say. Maybe I can talk to her? Maybe I can heal whatever soul-wound she's carrying from a war that was one or two generations before her? Maybe I can take her under my wing? Give her an internship? Save her life?

"Look. Boubacar. I don't know how to help you find what you're looking for. But if you do find her, tell her . . ." He pauses for a very long time. "Never mind."

I know better than to ask him to finish that sentence. He never will. Not until the day he dies.

But it does get the sand out of my sandals hearing Oumar talk the way he did just now. So when I get up and thank the nurses and walk out of the convalescent home, my back's a little straighter.

Soon as I leave the place, the air is warmer. The sun is brighter. The breeze is fresher. Oumar was talking in generalities, being all cryptic and whatnot, but he knew what I was talking about.

Maybe not the specific who, but he knows something's going on and that it's connected to that girl who stumbled into my place that night. Suddenly, I'm wondering why Moussa was after her in the first place. If there'd been some kind of terrorist attack, I would have heard about it. We all would. The policier are never shy about shouting their victories from the mountaintops. Maybe it was about the "will do" again. That future-tense headspace policier like Moussa have to live in. Maybe whatever the bad thing is hasn't happened yet. Which gets me walking even faster.

So fast that I run straight into someone's back.

It takes me a second to realize I'm on the outskirts of a large crowd. It's midday and this many people standing still in the middle of a street, this close to the city square, already has me worried. People should be working their shops. They should be getting ready to pick their kids up from school in a few hours. Life should be happening all around me right now. Loud and colorful, but it's all frozen. We're all frozen. And I see they're all staring at something raised over the central dais.

So I shrug and nudge and push my way through until I'm close enough to the front. And then I stop, because all the energy to take another step has evaporated.

Suspended in the air, rotating imperceptibly, is the girl. Jets and curtain rods of blood hanging in the air around her. Her back is arched, her legs dangling but not moving. Her face is angled toward the sun.

But the thing I can't help noticing, the thing that makes it all truly hurt, is that when whatever this is happened, she didn't have her sandals on. No one's ever looked as naked and as vulnerable as that girl held up by air, with nothing to cover her feet.

CHAPTER FIVE

When Moussa shows up in my doorway, he's got a new grayness to his skin. Of course he's seen it too.

Maybe he really did think he was gonna save that girl. Let him rot anyway.

"Those chairs are for clients only," I tell him.

He still sits down in one of them. Like he didn't even hear me.

"You here to tell me how I got that girl killed? How I shoulda just gotten out of your way and answered your questions straight-like? Because the last thing I need is for a client to walk through that door, thinking here's where they can find just a little bit of discretion, then see a policier sitting in their chair."

"Please," Moussa says. More tired than he's sounded in a long time. "Just shut up."

If he's playing for sympathy, he's got the . . . right idea. I shut up.

For a long time, he doesn't say anything. Then, he sits up and takes his fingers from his face. "What do you think?"

"What do you mean?"

"Of all of this. What do you make of it?"

"So, now you want my opinion."

"You're not working a case." There's still strong, steely warning in his voice. "But pretend like you are. What do you see?"

"I see a lot of question marks. What was she running from? Policier, for one."

"But you don't think that's enough."

"No. I don't."

"Hmm." Then, "What else?"

"Well, what the hell happened to her? Can't say I've seen that sort of thing every day. Hung up in the air like that. Floating."

"Maybe whoever she was running from finally caught up with her."

"What coulda done that to her?"

"Something mean."

"Dugu don't string up their kills like that. You know this, Moussa."

"I know," he says. More to himself than to me.

Something Moussa said during our last talk sticks with me. "You said you wanted to catch her 'before more français get involved.' What did you mean by that?"

"What?" Like he's waking up from a stupor.

"Who's already involved in this?"

He stares at me for a moment, then shakes his head. "There's no 'this' anymore. She's dead. Whatever we were after her for, we're not gonna get from her."

"This a hands-off type of deal? No touching the French? Moussa, if there are français involved in this, tell me now. That's a trail I can follow."

"Bouba, let me handle the French."

I want to make a crack about him doing a bang-up job of it so far, but that would be wrong. I'm not trying to hurt my friend.

"There is something you can do for me."

I try not to look too much like a dog waiting for his master to pet him. "Yeah?"

Then he hits me with something that snatches the air out of me. "This wasn't the first case."

"The first case of what?"

"Someone left to float."

For a while, I'm speechless. Too many thoughts spinning in my head, running up against stone walls, breaking apart. This doesn't make any sense. What does make sense is that Moussa would sit on this information until after it was absolutely necessary to tell me. He probably thinks that if I knew any earlier, I'd try to make a buck off of it. But these people, they're not missing. They're dead. And they're floating. Apparently. So, all I say is "Keep going."

"This one's number six."

"Number six?!"

"Number six."

Then a thought hits me. "Am I getting involved in some sort of cover-up?"

"No. It's not anything like that. Yet. It's just that . . . this is happening in the Ethnic Quarter. The outer arrondissements. Nobody cares about people dying in the outer arrondissements."

I still would've heard about it, though. Why didn't I hear about this until now?

"This one's different." Can't quite keep the growl out of my voice when I say it.

Moussa raises an eyebrow. "Different how?"

"Whoever did this put the body up in the city square. For everyone to see." I try not to let my anger show. Anger, the righteous kind, is rarely useful and always hypocritical. Being angry on behalf of someone, what good does it do? What good did it ever do? And I have to show Moussa that I'm not the type to let my emotions get in the way of my work. He may have even less reason to trust me if he sees that. "The girl was a trophy."

"You sure you haven't had any missing-persons cases recently?"

"No, Moussa, I'm broke on purpose. Of course I haven't had

any cases. No one related to the previous five came to me for help." I calm down. "Maybe they didn't want to raise any alarms."

"Maybe they have an idea of who's doing it."

"Well, then you have your lead. What do you need me for?"

"I can't go into the outer arrondissements. I'm policier."

"And they'll listen to me?"

"You're deux-fois. You speak their language. You're familiar with those neighborhoods."

"Just go on and say 'you're one of them.' I know you want to."

"You just said it for me. I'm not trying to be cute or beat around the bush here. If the dugu are being targeted and the killer's going public, this gets out of my hands quick-like. Help me keep it within the family."

"Whose family? Yours or mine?"

Moussa frowns.

"And what happens when they find out I used to be soro-dassi?"

"It won't come from me."

"Well, that puts my heart at ease. Some français hunting dugu, carving them up and putting them in the air, and you want to send a war vet into their world to ask them about it."

"Be serious, Bouba. You would've gone in anyway. You woulda sniffed this out before long, and the full might of the King's Army wouldn't have been able to stop you. Wolf with a bone."

"Difference is, I woulda been going in on my own terms. This way, I got no way of knowing what else you're holding out on."

Moussa relents, settles. "Okay, then. Another piece of info we gleaned from the murders—"

"So you're officially calling them murders?"

"Unofficially. Unofficially calling them murders."

"Of course."

"Another piece of info we gleaned is all the victims were missing some organ. Maybe the liver, maybe a kidney. Maybe both. Our coroners are still working the bodies. But, yeah. Everyone that was strung up like that was missing something in their stomach."

The woman appears before me in a flash. An apparition but full-bodied. Clenched in on herself like a fist. Gripping her stomach. Blood spilling through her fingers. Too little of it staining the floor. Was it floating too? Was she keeping it in the air? Moussa had said he'd followed her trail here, but there was no blood on the stairs. No blood in the street. Just the spot she'd left on my floor. "Your coroners. Could they tell if the organ was taken out before or after the victim died?"

Moussa raises an eyebrow. It hadn't occurred to him to ask that question. "We got no way of knowing that so far. Most of the victims have been dead too long for us to tell. And none of those organs have shown up." He shakes his head. "Not part of the trophy, I guess."

Oumar's too fresh a memory for me. So much of this crime work is context. But the war business is perspective. If there's a clash of peoples going on, then what's the big deal over one dead body? Five? Six? What do they matter? Those people never led an army. They were never going to be maire, never going to head an arrondissement. So why try to solve a murder when there are so many other dead bodies going around? But the war's over. This is supposed to be peacetime. I'm on the verge of some connection. A potential diéman killer targeting dugu. The Commission dredging up all that wartime shit. Elections coming up. These bodies moving more and more from the periphery to the center, from the colony to the metropole. Police, politics. Thread-ends about to touch, and I'm pulling with all my strength, but I can't quite tie it all together.

Moussa gets up to leave, but I'm not done with him just yet.

"Do you think you're the only policier on her case?"

"What do you mean?"

"When you said you were worried about more français being involved . . . did you mean other policier?"

"A cop didn't kill that girl."

His certainty startles me. He's too sure. "How do you know?"

"I know."

Well, maybe it was too much to hope that he would let something slip. But I can't rule it out. If the killer's diéman, well . . . there are plenty of diéman in the force. Maybe they've got help from ofisiden ye. But who else could move through the Ethnic Quarter and command such silence? Who else could scare these people so much that they crush out the very idea of gossip? Who else could kill a community so quietly?

Trying to answer these questions is what—

CHAPTER SIX

—leads me to Zoe's.

Before it was a shisha lounge, it was a teahouse, and, before that, it was a merchant stall. I never really knew Zoe as a kid. She was a little older than me. And because of where her parents were in the society scheme of things, she had to man the stall instead of going to school. Most folks in the produce business, they get left behind when city springs up behind them. It's a culture thing. Nobody sticks around long enough to impulse buy a thing or to reconsider prices because the person across from them is a familiar face. Not anymore. And that's why the fruit-sellers and all that lot get pushed into the outer arrondissements. If you can afford expensive silks in the city center, why would you bat flies away while perusing apricots in a next-door stall? The diéman prefer their apricots already prepared. They prefer apricot-flavored things. They wouldn't know the first thing to do with a fresh apricot.

But Zoe. Zoe was another story. I didn't see the transformation myself. But you walk through a space as commerce builds it up, changes it around you, and suddenly, the stalls have vanished, turned into storefronts. Mostly new faces, but a few persist. Zoe, a little bit older, serving tea to patrons sat on rugs, some of them wearing their fez, some of them in turbans still smelling of travel. Good spot for the nomads passing through. Also a good spot for the français who want a taste for the exotic. Gets tiring sitting in wooden chairs all day long. Sometimes, you want to stretch a leg out and lean on some cushions. And the women get to be flirted with by swarthy nomads or pretend-courted by adventurous dugulenw, while everyone knows the rules of the dance. Don't let their husbands detect any trace of you or that's your tongue or your fingers in the gutter. And that's what you get when the laws change, men and women filling the same space, danger bristling in the air between them when one's diéman and the other isn't.

With law-making comes law-bending, and brushing shoulders with the forbidden peoples grows into brushing shoulders with their forbidden imaginary customs. No dugulen smoked shisha before the French came, before the war, but the idea probably hit on Zoe that this was a market to be tapped into. And that's when the transformation completes itself. The market isn't the community. It isn't people you know walking by your stall, taking your harvest in their hands and weighing it. No, the market is something larger. Something it's impossible to wrap your arms around. The French blew up the market, and Zoe set up shop in the crater.

I know this makes it sound like I'm complaining, but I'm not.

If you come here during the day when people are usually out working, you can colonize a corner with some cushions and have a shisha pipe to yourself. The others spread out through the main lounge area stare off into the air, exhaling their apple-smelling clouds. Or they stare at the ground in front of them, contemplating the past or their future, their kids or when they were kids themselves. Or there's a small cluster of friends smoking together and chatting, playing a game of mancala, quietly arguing among themselves. Everyone respects everyone else.

Only thing is, as the market gets more invisible, so does Zoe.

Which is why I've had to just come by and hang out every day, smoking myself hoarse, for a week. Zoe would be able to answer my questions. No one's more plugged-in than her. But, if I'm honest, I haven't seen her face on purpose in years.

It's nice, though. Smoking. Easy to imagine us doing this sort of thing back in antiquity or whatever. The nomads were definitely on to something. It's the type of thing you can do with a group of friends. Also the type of thing you can do if you want to be left alone. Maybe I can buy a pipe and bring one to Oumar. Instead of tepid tea served by françaises, we could puff out these big, beautiful clouds of smoke. Smoking some shisha might even out Moussa while we're at it.

I'm mid-rumination when a heavy sits down in front of me.

The polite thing to do woulda been to say hi to me, at least pretend you were a gracious server or security guy checking in on a customer. But this one can't even be bothered to fake a smile.

"Can I get another set of coals?"

Him and his bald head don't say a word to me.

"It's getting a little harsh." I hand him the pipe so he can see for himself.

He doesn't move. Doesn't even smack my hand away for daring to be impertinent. "Let's go upstairs" is all he says. But he doesn't move.

"You leadin' the way, or should I—"

Now, he gets up. But he just stands over me, fists all balled up. And a part of me resigns myself to whatever fight's waiting for me "upstairs." So I lay the open end of my pipe on the metal ashtray under the bowl, creakingly push myself to my feet, then follow the heavy up the wooden stairs by a side wall.

Ain't a single pair of eyes following me. Everyone here seems very good at minding their own business.

"Upstairs" is, in many respects, just like the ground floor, but with wooden railing against which cushions are bunched.

In the far corner in an all-black agbada and slouching cap, arms stretched out, a shisha pipe between his legs, is Zanga.

"Boubacar," he says from behind his fresh shave. You can tell a man's low-level, front-facing crime by the way he grooms himself. If he's gotta be seen by people, he can't be seen looking haggard or unwashed. And he has to preen. It's how he gets people to respect him. That and the threat of violence. Those above him, they get seen only by who they want to be seen by. If they wear neatly trimmed goatees, it's because they like how it feels, not because other people like how it looks. But the goatee and the silver filigree of his agbada . . . he's not a heavy. He's head heavy. "Loyal customer Boubacar. Come." He pats the seat next to him.

I glance around at the heavies who've now filled up the place. Five in total. Then I look back at Zanga and take my seat next to him. Soon as I sit down, so do the others.

"I can't remember the last time you graced our establishment. And now here you are, for hours at a time, every day of the week, and you don't once come upstairs to greet me."

"Usually the host who offers kola, not the guest."

"Ah, you are right. But special rules for you, my friend. Special rules." The menace is too obvious in his voice. "Now, really. What are you doing here?"

"Work's been slow. Bills piling up. I'm not exactly gonna go to the opera now, am I?"

Zanga laughs, too loud. The others join in. I can only imagine what the guys downstairs are thinking. Maybe one of them is shaking his head in exasperation and sorrow, thinking to himself, "That poor bastard."

"Like you said. I haven't been back in too long. To be honest, don't know why I ever stopped coming."

"Maybe a lot of people went missing and you had to go find 'em. Eh?"

"Indeed." I reach for the tea on the table. The arm wrapped around the back of the couch wraps around my shoulder. I feel every muscle in that arm flexed against my back. The man could snap my neck right now if he wanted to. So I lean back, and he pats my back.

Then, to make a show of it, he takes the tea, refills his glass, then knocks it back. Slowly. Pours himself another, drinks. Then another. And drinks. When he sets the empty glass on the table, he does it so roughly even the tea leaves jump in it. "Look. Boubacar." He leans in, his mouth to my ear, like what he's about to say is for me to hear and me alone. Like this whole thing isn't a performance for all his goons. Just like that silver filigree and that goatee. "The only reason you're not a stain on my floor right now is that they'd hang me for killing a vet. Allah knows they'd hang me even if I didn't. So tell me. What are you doing here?" He's got his hand on the back of my neck now. Squeezing.

"I'm here about that dead girl."

For the briefest of moments, that grip loosens. But he's still holding me in place. "You think she was a customer?"

"I was gonna ask your bamuso."

"Well, Bamuso's not in today."

"You know when she'll be in?"

"Not while you're here." He lets me go roughly, then pushes me away.

That's my cue to get up. "So, was she?"

"Was what?"

"Was she a customer? The dead girl?"

"Get out of my sight."

I head past the first of the now-standing heavies. When I'm at the top of the stairs, I can tell Zanga's standing too. Something tells me to turn around.

"Actually," Zanga says, walking toward me, "you can do something for me. Might help you find out about that dead girl I don't know nothin' about."

"Yeah?"

"Fix a problem for me."

"I'm not a cop anymore."

"Even better."

CHAPTER SEVEN

Zanga's problem is a wagon.

They seat me up front with the horses and even put the reins in my hands. None too gently, of course. There's a tarp over the back. One of the heavies—the bald one—sits up front with me. Probably to keep me from looking back to see what they're loading onto the carriage. This case is important enough to me that I don't risk a backward look anyway. I want to see what's on the other end of this whole affair more than I want to see what's in that carriage. So risk has to take a backseat.

I can't really hear or smell whatever the stuff is either. Maybe it's wrapped up. Or maybe they did something to it. I can only feel the wagon jostle a little bit with each toss. But that's it. Then, two slaps on the carriage, and the bald heavy next to me gives me a perfunctory nod.

I slap the reins and we're off.

For a bit, we wind through the backstreets of the Ethnic Quarter, then we're out onto the crowded souq streets with the storefronts. Ain't a single diéman face to be seen. The souq in the daylight has the air of a place that's never known crime. Closest thing to a dugu that can exist in a city. Which is why it's on the outskirts. Everybody seems to know everybody else. Even where the vendor didn't watch the customer grow up or their parents or uncles or cousins didn't know each other personally, they haggle and shout and argue and smile and curse like family.

Can't remember the last time I was so surrounded by my

people. Then I'm reminded of something Zanga said before he put me on this wagon. Something he whispered in my ear just as I ascended.

"I lied," he told me. "You bein' cop or no cop's got nothing to do with this. Ofisiden ye won't stop you because you're deux-fois." And therein lies my usefulness.

Makes me look around with new eyes. No one notices our wagon rumbling through. How many times did ignoring a français save their lives? I got a little of the oppressor in me and these people here will go out of their way to not pay attention to what I'm doing. Flip that coral shell around when we leave the Ethnic Quarter.

The roads get wider, paved or at least partially paved. And guards wave me through without another glance. I got the nose and the forehead and the iris color that tells them I couldn't possibly be up to no good. Or, if I am, it's harmless French fun. Nothing that could possibly destabilize the colonial order. I'm what they call regime-friendly. At least, half of me is.

We get through another checkpoint. This time, it's Kingsguard. There's a whole traffic jam of wagons and people behind us. People the guard have to search or question. The shuffling of ID papers. The protests, the lack of protest. The conversations that get hushed whenever law enforcement walks by. We leave all that in our dust as soon as a guard sees my face, my features, and waves us out of the line into a shorter, faster queue, then through the gateway.

Now, the city square is in our view.

Can't see it and not think of that girl strung up like that on invisible ropes. Just hanging there. Slowly rotating like she'd been put in a display case. The place is only a little hushed, but people are still going about their business. Whatever it is people do here in the middle of a city. One thing I'll never stop noticing is how the paper here is all flat. People read the news on flat sheets they have to hold out instead of scrolls they unroll, and they just end up folding the thing end over end anyway. Holding the folded things in the crook of their arm. It's one of those little things— when you're so used to seeing scroll-ends poking out of satchels— that reminds you a place is changing. Or has changed.

"Crazy what happened, huh," I say to the heavy next to me. Silence.

"Just up there like that. How'd she get like that? You think it was some newfangled French technology? I mean, they're doing all kinds of things these days. I hear they've even got a railway going up north. There's talk of trams here. I mean, what are we gonna do with all these horses?"

He doesn't even frown. Doesn't budge. He's a piece of furniture on this bench next to me.

"Can you imagine what it'd be like to ride a tram? Just right through checkpoints like—"

A single shot to the kidney and I'm doubled over. Pain all through my side. Spreading to my stomach. My arm gets tight for some reason. It's like he collapsed everything inside me to the right of my spleen.

In my petty attempt at revenge, I lean on him so that it seems to anyone looking on that we're lovers. I can tell the physical contact is making the guy want to erupt, but he can't do what he wants while all these young français are near enough to see it. An ant-sized victory, but I'll take it. Almost worth the punch to begin with.

I start to get my wind back as we near Le Marais.

Tall greenery rises like a gate around us. A boundary. And just like that, all sound drops away.

The branches and leaves tower over us and all of a sudden, everything is straight paths and bubbling stone fountains where the paths meet. That gurgle is one of the only sounds to be heard.

Then the low murmur of French being spoken by diéman bundled up in all sorts of clothes. Jackets whose coats touch the calf. Women in white dresses with parasols to shield from a sun the trees hide them from anyway. It's all alien here, and it wasn't here the last time I was in this part of town. Or, at least, I don't remember it.

We skirt the homes. Apartment buildings where people live quite literally on top of each other. Everything stacked to the sky. Shingles, red tiles, winding sidewalks. It's pleasing to look at, the geometry of it, if you could call it that. But it feels cold. The temperature here is lower. Reminds me of Oumar's convalescent home. That's a power the diéman have somehow figured out. How to snatch the heat out of a place. Even during Harmattan season, it feels like it's just rained here.

But our jaunt through the French Quarter with its gardens and benches and apartment dwellings is short-lived. We're once again into open, treeless territory. The cobblestones and paved roads give way to dirt and rocks. Even the horses think this is more familiar footing. I barely need to drive this thing.

I don't realize I'm getting ready to lean back until the heavy next to me does something with his arm, his hand, something. And I get a sharp pain at the small of my back. Maybe he thought I was chancing a look at what's in the wagon behind us.

"I'm only stretching," I tell him.

"Stretch when we're done," he tells me.

Up ahead, a warehouse looms. More like a giant barn than anything else. Bigger than any barn anyone has any right to build. Or own, because I hardly think the diéman nailed the wood and put up the roof by themselves.

The heavy nudges my leg with his knee. That's my signal to slow down.

I pull up and a bunch of guys I don't recognize spill out of the giant warehouse. The land all around it is empty. There are mountains in the background. If you want to be isolated, you could do worse than sit yourself here. If you want to stick out, this is a pretty good spot too.

The new guys flank the horses and take the reins from me. The carriage is still moving. Slower, though. I make to hop down, but the heavy grabs my shirt like I'm a kid making trouble for his bamuso in the market.

It'd be helpful if the guy—any of them, really—would tell me what they want me to do. Get off, stay on. Don't look back, let go of the reins, drive the cart, sit still. I feel like a ball kicked around by a bunch of shebab fresh out of the madrasa.

We get to the back of the warehouse and that's when I'm practically tossed off my seat. I don't even try to land softly.

Now's my chance. While I'm down, the other heavies—practically covered in drapery and flowing cloth—move around me. Practically kick me out of the way. They get to the back and begin unloading. But before I get more than a glimpse of a coffin-looking thing, the bald heavy hauls me to my feet.

"Zanga'll pay you when you get back. Go on, now."

I don't know how long I stand there, but the other guy realizes after a bit that I'm staring at him. My mouth musta been open.

Turning, I want to tell him that I wasn't trying to sneak a peek. I was legitimately shocked. That was the most he said to me all in one go. Didn't think he had it in him.

I take about five steps, then pause.

"Hey," I tell him, "how am I gonna get back?"

The bald heavy looks at me for a very long time, silent. Then he looks at my sandaled feet. Then he looks back up at me.

So I head back to Zoe's—

CHAPTER EIGHT

—where about five of Zanga's goons beat the shit outta me.

CHAPTER NINE

There she is huddled against the back wall of my room. It's night. Moonlight hits the floor between me and her. She's still in darkness, except for a slice of light coming across her face. She's sweating. I could fill a dozen calabash bowls with what she's sweating. And she's got both hands pressed to her left side. That's where the blood's coming from. And that's where the blood hangs. Droplets of red. And other droplets attached like spiderweb to somewhere past her fingers, somewhere behind her skin. She's bleeding. She's not bleeding. Both at the same time. There's no urgency here. We just need to stay still. Everything will fix itself. There's no sound. But not because some dream-stuff is muffling the window. No. Everywhere is asleep. It's just us awake. The only people in the whole city with our eyes still open.

I want to walk to her. I don't want to walk to her. Both are happening inside me, but they're all tangled up. So instead, I knot up and just crouch on my haunches.

We're looking at each other. Staring. She's held my gaze the whole time. She's shivering. I think I want her to tell me what to do. But I'm not sure. My wants are all confused here. Sit down, stand up, let go of the reins, hold them tighter, move faster, slow down, heal me, harm me, kiss me, kill me. Better that I just do nothing.

"Are you jatigewalekela?" I ask her.

She doesn't look like she's any closer to speaking than she

was a minute ago. Just these heavy, shuddering breaths. Holding herself together with bloodstained hands.

"Is a diéman after you?"

Still, nothing.

"If a diéman is after you, I don't know that I can protect you. I don't know the escape routes anymore. I don't know the smugglers. Not the ones who would help you. Not the ones who owe me a favor, who'd do something like that for free. Not anymore. Those folks are gone. I don't know the hiding places either. I used to. I used to know where lovers hid from the prejudices of others. I used to know where they'd couple. I used to know where they'd set up a life for themselves, doing their best to live undisturbed. I used to know all that. But I don't anymore. I don't know anywhere you could go. If a diéman is after you . . . did you at least get a good shot in?"

Is that a glint of mischief in her eyes? Probably just a trick of the light.

I slide onto my backside so I'm sitting cross-legged across from her. A small mountain of chin-chin appears in my right hand. Without a second thought, I start popping them in my mouth. They have just the right amount of sweetness. The crunch is a pleasant distraction. "How are you doing that?"

She knows what I'm talking about, but she still holds out on me.

"How'd you leave so little blood on my floor? And how'd you leave none on the stairs on your way here?" I keep thinking that if I approach it from the side, I can get at an answer. I can get on the right track. But all I'm doing is making a fool of myself cutting through jungle and trying to stay on rabbit trails. Because at the center of it all is "Why me? Why did you come to me?" But I know the answer to that. It was an accident. Just happened to be me who lived here. The family on the ground floor woulda made too much ruckus. The ofisiden ye woulda found her in a second and a half. But it was quieter up here. That much, you can tell from the street. Rarely a light on in this room. Almost nobody who cares knows I live here. Maybe she thought this place was empty. A place to warehouse herself while the danger passed. Somewhere quiet where she could go about the business of holding her guts inside her.

She lets out a too-large sigh. Like she's deflating. Then that ragged quality leaves her breathing. She's breathing quiet now. Losing energy. She's dying. This isn't what happened.

"Help me here." And the words are already out of my mouth before I realize how stupid it sounds, asking a dying woman for help. Me on the shoreline asking the drowning lady to save my life.

The shivering hasn't stopped.

"Maybe I made you up. Maybe you're just a symbol." Now I'm starting to sound like Moussa. And I don't even have kids. But we're both here and not going anywhere anytime soon, so I pop more chin-chin in my mouth. "Maybe I made this whole thing up. Maybe this is what used to happen in the village when we said someone went mad. Started seeing what wasn't there. Talking to who wasn't there. Convinced there's this whole thing happening around them, this whole world they're living in filled with strangers and people they know, and only they can see it. Feel it. Maybe Moussa was talking to me about something else the whole time. Maybe you're just what my unresolved guilt looks like. A pretty girl with her gut cut open. It's a sick thing to say out loud, yeah. I know. But . . . I'm trying to be a better guy. I'm trying to do good. I've . . . that's what I've been trying to do. Helping people most others won't. Trying to . . . I don't know . . .

connect people. Or something like that. Everything's so big and anonymous now. No one knows anyone anymore. People moving away, getting new names, villages turning into neighborhoods turning into cities. I . . . can anyone keep up with that? It's all so fast. Is that what happened? The city tried to eat you?"

"Don't be stupid."

I sit up. What? Did she say something? No, that wasn't her voice. But how would I know what her voice sounds like? She maybe said a total of three words to me last time we were face-to-face and they were probably "help," "me," and "please." No, this voice is deeper.

To my left, suddenly, sits Oumar. Except, there's no chair. He's sitting on air and has an arm resting on a table that isn't there. He's not looking at me. He's looking at the girl.

Who's holding his stare.

He's got just as many wrinkles as the last time I saw him. And that snaps something in me, makes me remember where I am. That the girl isn't made-up. She's not the embodiment of my guilt. She's something that exists. Outside of me. At least, she did once upon a time.

"She probably had a family," Oumar says to me, even though he's still staring straight at the girl. "Maybe her fa was a brick-layer. Or a farmer. Maybe he was a mean son of a bitch. But maybe he looked at her as a baby and spoiled her rotten. And maybe her bamuso had a fire tongue. Or maybe she was the silent steel that held the home together, kept it running. Girl's got a rebellious streak in her. Maybe it's because of how much her fa loved her. Maybe it was her mother that nurtured it in her. Maybe both are true." Then he turns to me. Slowly. And he's got a sneer pulling at half his mouth. "All this time, you ain't once ask her about her family."

I get it. It hits me in my chest something fierce, but I get it.

Made this all about me, trying to reach inside her belly and pull out some personal redemption.

"You're losin' the plot, Boubacar." He nods at her. "That's a person there. She ain't a clue. She ain't a goal. And she ain't a mystery. That's all the other bullshit. This right here is a person."

And he's right. He's damn right. That's what I get for living in this business for so long. It turns people into work. Wives, husbands, kids, parents, bandits, fugitives, paramours, villains, pursuers, the powerful, the powerless, they all get turned into work soon enough. People that pay me, or don't. People I gotta find answers for, and it's always been about giving them the answer, filling in the void for them, but what I give them is never enough to fill up all that blank space. You can't replace a person with the memory of them. You can't replace a person with information.

"Bouba?"

My head's been bowed. But I raise it and look at the girl and she looks at me back.

"Bouba?"

"I think I'm done, Oumar," I tell him. "I think this is it. I'm not saying this is my last case. I'm saying I had my last case a long time ago. Maybe . . . I think I need to leave this one alone. Let it lie. Whoever's still alive to mourn her, they'll mourn her. It ain't . . . it ain't my business anymore."

"But it is." This time, it is her.

Slowly, she pushes herself to her feet, leaves a bloodsmear on my wall. Then she looks up, and all of a sudden my roof is gone. And so are the walls to my place. The girl keeps her eye trained on the sky, and it's day-blue now. Not a speck of sand in it. Then she starts to rise. Like the air's gently lifting her higher and higher. And her back starts to arch, and Oumar's tracing her flight pattern as well.

Until she's well above our heads, back arched, hands loose from her stomach, and the blood spills through the air and swims around her in tendrils.

"But it is," she says in that voice I can hear clear as day when I wake up.

CHAPTER TEN

I wake up needing to take a shit. First face I see when I open my eyes is Moussa.

The urge to get up is almost enough to get me to power through the hurt. I feel like I been caught in a Harmattan but the sandstorm was made out of fists and feet. Fingers bound together to look like claws, still throbbing at each joint. Can't open either eye all the way. Nose twisted, whole head wrapped up. Sounds coming through muffled because my ears are bandaged too. Don't know if I'll come out of this still being able to walk. But above all, I need to take a shit.

"I saw her," I tell Moussa. "She was right there."

"Saw who?"

The unreality of where I just was hits me right between my swollen eyes. "Never mind. Was just a dream." My words are slurred coming out. I think I might be missing some teeth.

I can't really see it, but I imagine Moussa's spending a moment or two looking my bandaged, poulticed body up and down, surveying the damage, and that he's got a little regret stuck in his teeth somewhere. Maybe he's wondering if anything useful came out of this. Maybe he regrets that my jaw's probably broken because I can't give him any intel. Maybe I'm not giving him enough credit. Maybe it actually pains him to see a friend like this.

I choke out a laugh. Making him feel bad is almost worth the twin pains in my jaw and my ribs.

"Sorry for sending you into the belly of the beast like that."

"You get what you wanted?"

"This ain't what I wanted."

"You sure?"

He looks hurt by that. Or doesn't. I still can't see too well. "What did I ever do to make you think that?"

Fair. So we sit in silence. Or, I assume Moussa's sitting. I'm lying down, and his voice sounds close. "So. Where am I?"

"Temple. Couldn't get you a private bed, so we're in the jawili."

"Shoulda brought me to where all the other weak-feet are. Them hard-of-hearing types can't listen in on what you probably wanna talk to me about."

"What I want is for you to get better."

And I got reason to believe him. The girl's dead. And the clues died with her. So did my desire to get to the bottom of it all.

"Truth is, I barely got anybody left doing real cop work."

"Police on strike?"

Which gets me a chuckle from Moussa. "No, they're doing election security. Damn politics stuff. Though, you ask them, it's the cushiest gig they could ever hope for. Stand around the centre-ville where all the diéman live and stare down anybody who looks suspicious."

"Anyone who looks dugu."

"Same thing."

"You still wearing your fez or have you let your hair fall like a true français?"

Moussa grunts.

"More than one way to be deux-fois, you know."

And I know he knows what I mean because he's silent for a long time. Don't like what I'm suggesting, that dressing like he can move between both worlds isn't the same as being deux-fois on the inside. He'll always be a tourist, and he's mad at me for it. Is that why he sent me into what he called the belly of the beast? Hell of a way to treat a friend.

"I ain't mean it like that," I lie.

"Sure, Bouba." But now his quiet has that dangerous pensiveness to it.

"What'd they do with the body?" I ask him, in part to get him out of his head. In part so he stops trying to figure out another way to hurt me. Not like I can defend myself in my current state.

"You think there's some deeper meaning to what happened to her?"

Which doesn't answer my question but is an interesting enough thread to pull.

"I'm not talking about her killer sending a message. I'm talking . . . the horror of it. It gave me this feeling, seeing it. Like I was being pushed outside myself. Toward something bigger than myself."

You're starting to sound like a killer, I want to tell him. But I keep my mouth shut. Still hurts to talk too much.

"It was . . ."

"Horror?"

"No. I see horror all the time. Violated bodies, what a long time in jail does to someone who's not built for it. I seen what the français sometimes do to the dugu because they know they can get away with it. We saw horror when we were in the sorodassi together. That stuff just numbs you. Shock. Revulsion. All that. Then you get to the business of it. That's what it becomes. Business as usual. Stay in it long enough, and it's just weather. The changing of the seasons. This . . . what I'm talking about is different. It's . . . I dunno, the unseen?"

"Terror?"

He turns to look at me, which is how I know he's been looking at something else this whole time. "Yeah. Terror."

It's the first time I wonder if Moussa's haunted by the same stuff I'm haunted by. Does he dream about her? Like I did? Does he still think about the sorodassi and what we did? Is his work wearing him down? Something pinches my heart. I care about him. I don't want to see him suffer. Well, half see. My eyes are still swollen shut.

"I'm standing there, looking at this dead body floating in the air for everyone to see and, get this, I feel like something horrible is *about* to happen. I'm looking at the horrible thing and yet it feels like something different, something worse, like that's right around the corner. Horror's seeing the dead body. Terror's the smell of a dead body in the air, right before you find it."

"Terror's getting someone to hang a body in the air with no rope."

"I wasn't scared. I . . . it was just that I was looking at something that shouldn't be. She wasn't doing anything. Wasn't saying anything. She was just this . . . this violation of . . . the world."

"Sounds like more than police work."

"Maybe it is."

"Maybe it isn't." Her face, her body, in my dream. It's the clearest image in my head right now. "Maybe she was just a person who got the bad end of a thing." She's not a symbol, I want to tell him, but my lips are cracked again. "Water."

"Huh?"

"Water," I croak.

And Moussa obliges. He probably had to go somewhere for it, but he's back a minute or two later and he slowly lifts me up and puts the small dish to my lips. Best drink of water I've ever had.

"Mmm." I cough. "Thanks." Moussa's making me think that

maybe this is what the murderer was after. Not just killing a person, but destabilizing a society. A whole order. How Moussa feels, is that how the diéman feel? If a français did this, were they sending a message to their race-fellows? What message? Maybe that's why our word for them sounds so much like the French word for demon. In the end, perhaps that's what this murderer is. A demon. I want to say all this to Moussa, but it would involve me having to clarify. I'd have to tell him that whatever did this probably doesn't have a tail. Probably doesn't have fangs either. It's not a what. They're a who. Machines don't build monuments. People do. That's what the killer was trying to do with that girl. Turn her into a monument. "You think there's anyone out there . . . who misses her?"

I can tell from how long he pauses that Moussa hasn't asked himself that question before. Or maybe he knows the answer and is trying to spare me. But I can't tell what would be worse. That there's a family out there with a hole in it the size and shape of her? Or that there's no one, truly no one, who cared enough about her to miss her. Maybe anyone fitting that description is dead.

"I need to get out."

"You got at least a month in here before you'll even be able to eat properly again. You're not going anywhere. If anything—"

A week is more like it. I can't fault him for caring. "No. I mean . . . I need to get out of the business. I was wrong."

"Wrong about?" But he knows what I mean.

"This is all wrong. It's . . . it's turning me into . . . my mind's all . . . it's gotten too dark."

"Back to that 'this ain't my business' schtick?"

"No, it ain't that. It's just . . . I don't like what my job's turning me into. Ain't natural. To be pushed up against the worst of what we do for so long. So often. Got my face up against the glass, had it that way for years. Too many years. It's time to stop. Can't save that girl if she's already dead."

I think Moussa's actually shocked because for a long time, he lets me sit (or lie down) in the quiet. Maybe he's frustrated. Maybe he's disappointed. Maybe he's relieved.

"I think I wanna move somewhere. Find an empty spot, refurbish an apartment. Sneak my deux-fois ass into the French Quarter."

Moussa's chuckle surprises him, so it comes out half choke. "With what money?"

I make to shrug, but the gesture's so small because of the pain that I don't think he notices.

"Why not build something on your own? You could find an open plot of land, get all the materials yourself. You wouldn't have to pay anyone with all that money you don't have."

"How?"

"How what?"

"How do I find a free plot? The French have bought up everything."

Through the slit of my eyes, I see Moussa stroke his chin. "Property records are public at the Mize. You could check there. See who owns what. One thing about the French, there's a record of everything."

I laugh as much as I'm able to. "You and I both know that's a damn lie."

This whole thing, a damn lie.

CHAPTER ELEVEN

A damn lie.

Because the first thing I do when I'm strong enough to stand upright and do little else is stumble to the Mize to find out who owns that warehouse I brought that wagon to.

I have to walk with a cane. That doesn't mean I can't see the hooded figure following me from a discreet distance. But it does mean I can't outrun him. Can't circle the block. Can't sneak up on him. So I'm just out here, ineptly threading my way through crowds while my cane click-clacks on the cobblestones. It would make a nice weapon, though. That thought makes me feel a little better. Still, it ain't outside the realm of possibility that I'm dealing with a mogofagala. Why do I say that? Especially when mogofagala are known to live and work in shadows? When they only ever poke out to leave a dead body in their wake? Well, they got a knack for anonymity. In the wide-open savannah, back when the dugu was the only place where people went about the business of living, the mogofagala were called all sorts of things. Allah's vengeance on wrongdoers. The workings of the weather. Like a well-placed lightning strike or a hidden pit of quicksand. The universe's caprice. Or just plain bad luck.

Here, in the city, they still got some of that mystique. They keep their reps nice and polished. Piece of construction falls on an unsuspecting pedestrian? Bad luck. Sounds more romantic to say mogofagala. Robbery gone wrong? Maybe the mogofagala just made it up to look like a robbery. Maybe the dead guy or gal was on the bad end of a vendetta. Bad blood now inching in a pool out the mouth of an alley.

Mogofagala would be a noble way to go out. The thought's got me thinking I'm way more important than I might actually be. They're not cheap. And I don't think I've kicked a large enough wasp's nest. Yet.

The Temple's on the other side of the city from the Mize, so I have plenty of chances to scope out this maybe-mogofagala. White hood, which is not a bad choice with how bright the sun's shining. There might be a bit of shimmer in the thread. That bit about lightning striking was literal. There's a little bit of color in the robe, bits of red and gold. I catch a glimpse of hands. A little bit of cheek escaping shadow. White. Clever. Could be a mask or scarf around the face. Gloves on the hands. If I go down, they'll say français did it. If I go down, they'll say I had it coming. Cleaner than the guillotine.

I've got an idea.

The Temple abuts the Ethnic Quarter, far from L'Hôpital, where français get treated if a private doctor isn't doing the trick. But if I wind my way out of the commercial districts and through the more residential areas, where the madrasas start to turn into écoles, I can get a look at voting booths. I got the idea from what Moussa mentioned. About losing his cops to election detail. It's a dangerous idea, and it'll take me longer to get to the Mize. But it's the best idea I've got so far.

And sure enough, ofisiden ye try not to be awkward next to French cops while election officials set up their booths. They kinda look like merchant stalls. Dugu laborers nail together painted signs, carry table legs, all of that.

I try to look as natural walking by as I can. Don't want them to think I'm casing the joint. The French know that whichever way things go, they're safe. But the king has a vested interest in making sure these things happen without a hitch. Don't want the people thinking he's an illegitimate protector. But that's probably the wrong way to think about it. King doesn't wanna impress his people. He wants to impress the French. And that'll take a hit if word gets out that some deux-fois with a cane looks like he's up to something suspicious. Maybe this ballot-stuffer is putting on an act, they'll say once I'm in jail or on my way up to the guillotine. Who knows what he was hiding in that smelly djellaba of his? Then that's my head in a basket while the populace praises the king and the French government.

A chance look over my shoulder and the hooded figure is still trailing me. There are fewer people here, there's more empty space between us. But he maintains his distance. He's got something, a book or a tablet or something, in the crook of his arm. What the hell is his disguise?

If the ofisiden ye eye me from time to time, neither set of cops pays the guy following me any mind. So much for my plan.

You know what? Maybe this is just some sort of intimidation. But who shells out for mogofagala just to have them not go all the way? Only the français have that kind of money. And if they think intimidation's gonna work, they shoulda seen me get worked over by Zanga's boys. If that can't stop me, some scary mogofagala who won't even pull the trigger doesn't stand a chance.

Through the tops of buildings towering over me, I catch the spire of the Mize. Enough of drawing this out.

The Mize's probably one of the only spots near the French Quarter where you'll still see dugulenw. But it's a special type of dugulen. Professional dugulenw, dugu scholars. The type of dugulenw who work in French buildings, either for or alongside français. Mostly for. The gears that keep the universities running. But I guess the French liked the way we organize our records, so they left that mostly intact.

No cowrie shells or beaded necklaces here, though. If any of the staff wear jewelry, it's hidden or out of the way. An ear stud hidden by the flaps of a cap. A bit of shoulder chain running across exposed collarbone. That sort of thing. Instead, it's all pantalon and chemise or robe or veste.

I get to the bit of yard before the giant wooden doors of the Mize—a single tower with spokes poking out and bridges leading to other smaller towers—and the place starts to slowly clear out.

It's the type of clearing out that charges the air.

Immediately, I'm on edge. I taste electricity.

No one told these people to scatter, and they're not exactly in a hurry, but there's a lot more exposed ground now than there was a couple moments before. A quick glance over my shoulder, then a double-take. The hooded figure is gone. No mogofagala in sight.

Maybe I'm lucky. Maybe they got scared away.

It's quiet. A dry wind blows dust between me and the Mize. Might as well get after what's waiting for me in there.

The doors are slightly open. I can hear hushed activity coming from inside. A part of me wonders if my bad luck's run out. This is balancing at work. Get worked over by Zanga, get an easy path to these property records.

But just as I get within whisper distance of the place, a marabaga slides through the crack in the door and stands in my path. All black robes with gold rope cinching the waist, black braids coming down her back and over her shoulders, their edges ringed with gold. We're probably the same height, but the way she looks at me, she might as well be as tall as that Mize tower.

She doesn't say a word to me.

I meet her eye, then try to sneak past. An arm bars my path.

"Your card, Monsieur."

Ah, there it is. "Monsieur" from a dugulen. Looks like this is a French institution now.

"Your card," she says again.

I pat myself in front of the librarian. Make a show of it too like I actually have whatever the hell it is she's asking for. "I live across town, Marabaga. By the time I go home to get it and come back, the moon'll be out and the Mize's doors will be closed."

She frowns.

"Please. I just need to access some records. You won't hear a peep outta me. I'll be quiet as a village child after a whooping." To sprinkle a little sugar on it, I lean on my cane. Make it look like I can barely stand upright. "I've walked a long way, Marabaga. It is not an easy journey." With my free hand, I indicate the cane, itself not a pretty thing.

"Your card, Monsieur."

I raise my head, play with the angles a little. We're in the building's shadow, but maybe if I can catch the sun the right way, she can see the français in me. While I'm twitching my head back and forth, others are streaming into the Mize. They each absently flash the wooden talismans attached to their belts and head in without a word. The marabaga glances at a few and smiles, welcomes them. Repeat visitors. All while I'm trying to get this woman to treat me like she would treat any other français. "Please, Marabaga."

"Without your library card, I cannot let you in. Please come back when you have it in your possession." She peeks out over my shoulder, then looks back at me. "Bonne journée." Then she's back inside and the door's shut in my face. Not even a "Monsieur" this time.

"Hmmph."

Up the walls, the pegs catch the sun and silhouette. It's imposing from this angle. Makes the tower look like it goes on forever.

I've got my neck craned up when something brushes up against my leg.

I'm not fast enough to stop a cutpurse, so I don't even bother.

"They're all like that." It's a kid. He's got a tiny puff of hair around his head. He wears little more than a blanket with a hole cut in it for his head and a thin rope around his waist. I can tell already this kid knows his way around the city. He's got the callused hands for it. And the bottoms of his feet in his sandals are probably filthy. "There's no use hoping another one will treat you different."

"That so?" I'm already turning to head back the way I came. The kid's still at my side, keeping pace with single strides. He's antsy. I bet he wishes I could move faster. "Look, what do you want, kid?"

"The question is, what do you want?"

"That's what I said."

"No, I'm asking you. What do you want?"

"What's it to you?"

He nods at the Mize's main tower. "If it's in there, I can get it for you."

"You ain't once called me 'Monsieur,' you know that? You should respect your elders."

"What do you mean? I do respect my elders. I saw that cane and said to myself, that man needs my help. Then I saw the pitiful look on your face, and I said to myself, that man really needs my help. How could I go to sleep at night knowing that one of my elders was wandering the city lost and alone and I could have helped him but didn't?"

"Who said I was lost and alone?"

But the kid just shrugs.

"Okay, urchin. Start talking. How you gonna help me get what's in that Mize?"

CHAPTER TWELVE

"The first thing you need to know," the urchin tells me, "is that this is a team job."

I'm leaned against one wall of the back alley. The kid is on his haunches and, with a finger, he's drawing a diagram in the dirt. He's in shadows, but the drawing's in the light so it looks like some disembodied pointing finger's bringing this mini-Mize to life in front of me.

"It may look like a regular building on the outside, but that's just a disguise. On the outside, it's a regular dugu building. On the inside, a maze and a fortress."

"Tell me something I don't know, kid."

He looks up, and in the dark, I can see a pair of eyes glaring twin daggers the color of wet soil at me. "Fine. They keep property records on the top floor. If you're inside, you can only access them via an elevator they use ropes to operate. It can hold the weight of two grown men. Anything more, it strains the workers. And they can tell if there's added weight on there. So if you're thinking, 'oh send someone in with a little urchin in their sack,' they'll know how much a human weighs and then both are banned. For life."

"Okay, top floor." I shift against the wall. My shoulder itches. "Climb the spokes, then go in through the ceiling."

"Except the top of the main tower is surrounded by barbed wire."

"Barbed . . . how do you know?"

The urchin shows me both palms. That's answer enough.

"So, you're saying the mission's impossible."

"I'm saying that I don't want to go up in a puff of smoke."

I raise an eyebrow in question.

"The bridges linking the towers are also rigged with explosives."

This shocks me. "They'd blow up the Mize?"

"They have librarians working around the clock duplicating documents for storage in diéman facilities. That's why they can afford to lose records here."

I'm afraid to ask the next question. "How many dugu records are they duplicating?"

"Only documents in français. They don't care about losing dugu history. They don't care about dugu history period." For an urchin, he sounds real broken up about this. Gives me hope in the children and them wanting to keep their history, their culture, alive. Maybe they aren't all trying to turn white.

"Back to this being a team job. All I'm hearing so far is how you can't sneak in."

"I'm getting to that. I'm only saying that their fortifications are done in a way that they expect you to go through the top. But you play to that expectation. I have a climber in my crew—"

I look up instinctively. Half expecting the climber to dart over the alleyway between roofs, a dramatic silhouette announcing the arrival of a new team member. But there's only sunlight in sliver.

"He's good. Nimble. And reckless. He doesn't mind triggering the defenses and he—"

An idea hits me.

"Why not steal a library card and just hand it to me?"

The kid sits back and stops sketching. And for a long time, he looks at me with his head perched to the side. Like I've just revealed myself to be a dodo. Or like I've suddenly taken off my skin and inside me all along has been a baboon. It's not a mean stare. But it gets me to shut up.

"Anyway. You have to be strategic about the explosions you trigger. Because, as you know, you don't want to damage anything important. Another kid on my team, she's our demolitions expert. She knows how these things are wired. Even though they switch things up on us, she learns quick and we're always scouting the place so we can tell what their scheme is. Also"—he looks up from his drawing—"this isn't the only building in the city wired like this."

"What are you saying?"

"I'm saying we get plenty of practice."

I gulp. Suddenly, I'm nervous. How many buildings have I just been walking in or walking past that coulda blown me to bits without me even knowing. Then a more sinister thought creeps into me. Oumar had his house blown up. Wasn't the French that did it. Suddenly, the kid in front of me don't seem so harmless.

"The name of the game is distraction."

"I've seen plenty of magic tricks. Get the mark to pay attention to the right hand so they don't notice the left hand in your pocket."

The urchin smirks. "We trigger explosions in one place—a harmless place, maybe somewhere where duplicated French documents are already sitting—while the other explosives are disabled. They won't be guarding that because they'll be chasing our friend. The folks inside will still be manning the elevators, though."

"So how do you get past those?"

The urchin flashes too-white teeth. "We disable them."

"How's that?"

"You think we have just one kid at the explosion?" He's too

happy at this part. "Others climb over and smuggle some rubble into sacks that they then hand over to another team member in the courtyard."

"How's that kid get into the courtyard?"

"Tunnels. You didn't know about the tunnels?"

"Tunnels?!"

The urchin slaps his forehead like I'm the stupidest goat-looking guy on the planet. "Are you even from this city? The tunnels! How do you think the rebels fought off the French here and secured their homes?"

Then it hits me. Smart as this kid is, he can't tell I'm deux-fois. He thinks I'm dugu. Thinks I got a war wound and that's why I use this cane. Has no idea I fought for the other side. Smart kid. Dumb as shit too.

"We sneak the rocks in on the elevator. During an attack on the Mize, they block off the stairs. We load the rocks onto the elevator so they can't move, then we cut the rope." You can tell this is the part where he has the most fun. "Grab the rope and it shoots you all the way to the top. Feu d'artifice! We always draw sticks to see who gets to do that part. Because I'm Team Captain, I always win. Really, we are just seeing who is going to be my partner for this part."

"Okay, so you get to the top floor. Then what?"

"Well, then we get out, dummy."

"Oh, of course. You get out. How could I be so stupid?"

But he doesn't appreciate my sarcasm. "Then we hold on to the goods until we get the rest of our payment."

He relaxes, leans back on his hands, and I look at the full diagram he's sketched out. It's got the whole Mize facility as seen from above with arrows pointing in every direction and a bunch of scatter marks where the explosion is. There are zoomed-in parts to indicate the elevators and little dig-ins for the guards and dugu numbering along the side of the diagram too. This kid would grow up to be an engineer if he weren't dugu. Hell, he'd probably build a whole city if he weren't dugu. But he's got his color and swift, easy hands, so he steals things for people.

"How do you know I won't go to the Kingsguard or the cops with this?"

There's steel in his gaze like a flash. Like a wrist-flick to reveal a dagger. "We'd kill you before you got halfway to the gendarmerie."

"You ain't never killed anything bigger than a fly."

"A fly never threatened to get me into trouble."

"Fair."

"So!" He claps his hands together. "Let's talk rates. This consultation is part of our fee so we will be expecting a payment of—"

"Whoa whoa whoa. Slow down now. I haven't even said 'yes you're hired.'"

"But you're going to."

"How do I know this isn't your whole schtick, huh? Find unsuspecting joes, then tell them some crazy, made-up scheme about how you're going to break into fortified buildings and steal things for them, charge them for your 'consultation' then leave, huh? It's a pretty neat con. Wish I'd thought of it myself. Only problem is I got an office, so people know where to find me. And you don't. Pretty clever."

"The city is our office."

"Right." I put my fingers to my chin like I'm mulling things over.

"Be quick. They switch up their explosives and replace the ropes regularly, so if you're not fast, I'll have to do this all over again."

"And charge me for another 'consultation.' Right. I get it." I drum my fingers against my chin. "Let me think."

"Look. I know you're looking for property records. That means you've got your eye on some land. And you wanna buy it. If you don't have the money, then the guy behind you has money. Maybe I should talk to him."

"What makes you think I have a backer?"

"No. I mean the guy behind you."

"What?"

I turn and see him. He's standing in the light, not the shadows. Which doesn't make sense for mogofagala. But I'm sure there's plenty they're up to that will forever be far beyond my understanding.

"Monsieur Boubacar ———, I would like to talk to you," he says in the creepiest voice I've ever heard, "about your financial situation."

CHAPTER THIRTEEN

The face that appears when the figure at the mouth of the alley pulls back his hood is wrinkled like a date. But the color of fuzzy mold. And it's then that I see the rings. Black bands on the thumbs and pinkies. And a red band on the left middle finger.

Worse than a mogofagala.

A debt collector.

"I hope you are aware, Monsieur, that you are currently six months in arrears. We have sent several notices to the address we have on file."

The address they have on file? Maybe those kids the urchin was talking about can blow up the part of the Mize that's got my home address in it.

"As I'm sure you know, the rate at which your interest accrues has—"

"Yeah, yeah," I say, more to stop hearing that awful papery, snake-skin voice than anything else, "I know. Interest rates, amortization, sliding scale, all that complicated français jargon, all of that. I been meaning to get back to you, I just . . ."

"Well, Monsieur, in the event of continued nonpayment, we have sent, in accordance with our notification requirements, our intent to seize on your collateral property in order to secure payment contributing to your loan balance."

"I went to school, so you're gonna take my home?"

The loan officer looks taken aback. "Well, that isn't exactly how—"

"That's not how you'd put it?"

"Well, as we understand it, your office space is managed separately from your dwelling space, so the two would be treated—"

"You gotta be kidding me." I turn to face him fully and it takes me a good couple of seconds because my hips are still a little out of joint from the beating I took. "You don't see this?" I shake my cane at him and spread my arms to indicate the whole of my beat-to-shit self. But when I start to lose my balance, I put my cane down to lean on it again. "I'm old." A lie. "I can barely walk." Pretty true. "Do I look like I can pay your damn interest fees right now?"

"You can't pay your school fees?!"

I whirl back around and I see the urchin is still where I left him, crouched on his haunches, staring at me with his head cocked to the side like a damn bird.

"How were you going to pay for your consultation?"

"Hey, kid. I never said I was going to pay for no damn consultation."

"Monsieur," from the loan officer, "I would be more than happy to review with you our refinancing options."

"Refinance my ass!"

The urchin: "You should listen to the white man, you broke bum."

"Hey! Who are you calling a bum? Do you see your sandals?"

"My straps still work, you bum!"

"As I was saying," from the loan officer, "refinancing has worked for several of our prior—"

The urchin whispers under his breath but still loud enough for me to hear, "Wants to buy French property, wants to look at records, wants to hire a crew to steal them for him but can't even pay off his school fees. Buy property with what money?"

"What money is none of your business, kid. Now, Mister Loan Officer, I really don't—"

"Any property subsequently purchased while you are in arrears, Monsieur, would be seized and contributed to the amelioration of your loan balance."

"Enough about my loan balance, already!"

"But, sir, your total has reached a worrying height and—"

"And there's no way to stop it, is there?"

"Well, if you would make payments, it would lower your interest amount so that when the amortization period arrives, there would be—"

"He should try to amortize a wife," the urchin snickers.

"You don't even know what that word means, kid. Hell if you've seen a classroom in your entire life."

"Are you calling me stupid? You goat-looking bum? You goat-looking, weak-feet, bowlegged, only-has-one-djellaba-in-the-closet-lookin' bum?"

"With an interest rate currently at eight percent and scheduled to increase to nine in three days—"

"Poorhouse, color-of-shit-when-I-drink-cow's-milk-lookin' bum—"

"Your total will exceed—"

"None-of-your-children-ever-see-you-because-your-breath-stinks-lookin' bum. Broken-straps-on-your-sandals-lookin' bum, hairline-like-a-dirty-football-pitch-lookin' bum."

"With kaso as a last resort, but we wouldn't want to resort to—"

"I oughta slap the shit outta you if I didn't think I would catch your debt too. Contagious-bad-luck-lookin' bum."

"But of course we would only involve law enforcement as an absolute last resort."

"You really goin' to the kaso over school debt? Allah. Never known a broker bum in my life!"

"I'm not exactly supposed to tell you this as they discourage it at my place of employ, but it is possible for you to seek re-lief at the almshouse. Plenty of charities there that are willing to consider cases such as yours. The province of the Church. But I know sometimes people can be a little skittish about accepting from a God to which they don't—"

"I oughta rob you myself. Sleep-for-dinner-lookin' bum. I can't believe this."

I can't take it anymore, so I just lean back against the wall of the alley with my head in my hands and slide down. It's too much. A dugu urchin on one side roasting me with hellfire and opposite him, a loan officer threatening me with a kaso sentence because I can't pay for the schooling the army told me was free. And in two different languages too. So to the loan officer, it looks like the urchin's shouting gibberish to me. And to the urchin, all the loan officer's talk of interest rates and amortization probably sounds just as much like nonsense and baby talk. And here I am, cursed with the ability to understand both of these predators.

You could call it the Scourge of the Deux-Fois. It's not a mat-ter of being torn between communities. You look a certain way, you just pick one, and you stay as best you can. No, it's the fact that you can understand abuse in each language. They're always saying something bad about some part of you. They're always saying something bad to some part of you. And if you're one or the other, you can pretend at least not to understand it. You can call the other side crazy or ignorant or assume they have no idea what they're talking about. But when both ears are open, you can hear just how sophisticated the other side is, how cutting the insult. You understand that they understand more of your situ-ation than they let on. If you're barefoot, they don't just say it's because you can't afford sandals. They don't just say it's because you're too ignorant to fashion your own. They say it's because you sit in a particular seat in society, a specific room, and because things are the way they are, you're never getting out of that room. A français can look at the Ethnic Quarter and call it jail, even though it may not feel like jail to the people living there. But they know that the second a dugulen sees how the français live, they'll know the Twentieth for the jail it is. And the dugulenw know that français are nothing without their guns and without their stupid systems of paying for things, their overcomplicated ways of living. They know the français wouldn't stand a chance in a fair fight. That if it came to just the two of them in the middle of the savannah, only one of them is making it out alive. But the français can pretend not to understand what the dugulenw say about them.

They've closed in. The urchin and the loan officer. Right in each ear. The urchin's spittle hits my cheek. The loan officer's breath nearly doubles me over. I want to shrink in on myself. Just get smaller and smaller and smaller. So small I can sneak into a hole in the wall and get away. Or maybe just get so small I turn into a bug that can scurry through their legs and out the alley.

I'm entertaining my bug fantasy when the explosion throws us all to the ground.

It's a thunderclap. Also feels like a giant hand came out of the sky and swatted us all in the back of the head at the same time. Then kept pressing down.

The ground's rumbling so long that I chance a look up to see if the alley's gonna fall on us. The urchin's long gone but before he split, I saw the look in his eyes. First time I've ever seen him scared.

With almighty effort, I peel myself off the still-shaky ground and stumble over to the loan officer, who's curled in on himself. Notebook and pens and all that spilled on the ground around him.

"C'mon, buddy," I say, tired. And help/haul him to his feet so that we don't have both walls of this thing bury us alive.

What I see when we get into the square knocks my soul right out of my body. The loan officer collapses too. If the urchin sees this, he's probably doing the same.

It's half the French Quarter.

Floating in the air.

CHAPTER FOURTEEN

You can see it framing the Mize. On both sides, the trees that lined pathways hang at diagonal angles surrounded by dislodged cobblestones. The smaller pieces of stone and the larger chunks of pathway, they orbit the larger pieces—the trees, the shingled half-roofs. And then there are the apartments that have been lifted up into the air and tipped toward their sides. Whatever caused the explosion took out their façades. So you walk a little closer and you can see the kitchen. You can see the water hanging mid-gush from dislodged piping in people's water closets. Metal pots and pans from kitchens that can't do a damn thing about their newly nude status. Get a little closer and you can see the hands attached to those pot handles. You can see the disembodied legs hanging among the cobblestones and frozen columns of dirt that must have erupted from the ground. Get a little closer to where the erupted French Quarter practically hangs overhead, casts you and all the other spectators—some bleeding, some wounded in more invisible ways—in shadow, and you can see the bodies.

Some of the residents are caught mid-reaction to the explosion. Maybe they saw a flash of light. Maybe the ground fell out from under them before rocketing them up into the sky. Maybe the boom snatched their hearing from them, and the end of the world happened in complete silence. But for those that felt it somehow, somewhere in their bodies, there's that open-mouth shock on their faces. A grimace for some. A snapshot of grieving for others. Maybe a moment of rage in someone's graying face. One father clutches what looks like was once his son to his chest, buries the kid in the folds of his heart. Now that face is fused together with his father's chemise. A skinny, pretty much skeletal mother has her arms raised before her. Her face is turned away. She floats horizontal to the ground so it looks like she's afraid of the ground. Which makes sense.

Above me, right above me, a kid—same age as the urchin, looks like—fixes his eyes on me. He can't move his mouth. Crystalline red floats in streams from it like tributaries from a pond. He looks at me and his lips move. They disturb the blood-rivers just a little bit. But no sound comes out. Then he coughs. It's a small thing. More a puff than anything else. But right after, the kid's eyes roll back into his head.

There's a piece of wooden bedpost stuck right through his stomach.

That's when I hear—we hear—the first cry. It comes from a French woman a hundred paces ahead.

She's got on a white apron over a black dress. The apron's dotted with ash and soot. She must've been at an oven or furnace when it happened. And somehow for reasons none of us can guess at, reasons she'll spend the rest of her life wondering at, she was spared. But now, she looks at something or someone I can't see, someone blocked by detritus, and screams. All them choked-in sobs from before, it all comes out in some animal keen. I've seen diéman make a lot of noises in my life—booming laughs, sly chuckles, sucked teeth, sniffed sobs, death rattles—but I've never heard a diéman sound like this.

Then it's a chorus of them. Moaning, shrieking. I spent a couple nights in a forest when I was younger. Alone, little. Surrounded by all the things I couldn't see. And the bugs were singing and the night birds were singing and the wolves were singing. They were all calling. To each other. Past each other. But it was music. This, this is animal noise with no agreement, no melody, no harmony. It's just grief and it washes a wave like an aftershock over me.

Then a rumble behind me. More a bed of hushed whispers.

It's all dugulenw. Dressed in various states of assimilation. Some of them got the dark skin of their necks poking out from their white French collars or the black of the clergy. Others wear the type of djellaba and tarboush you see in the Ethnic Quarter. And there's every shade in between. Most of them look up at the mess in absolute shock, hands to their mouths. Some whisper prayers behind their fingers. But in some of their eyes is a dangerous glint. The look that says the French had this coming, whatever this is. That something cosmic has come to balance the ledgers of a people obsessed with crédits and débits.

Of course they musta heard the explosion from all the way across town. It's still surprising that they crossed the whole city so fast. Some of them look like they ran. But some look like they musta come from around the corner.

I wonder how many of them checked their own homes before coming here. Their own businesses, their own schools. Their own kids. Their own families. Rushed to local temples or market stalls or shisha lounges, looking for loved ones they'd said "n taara" to just that morning. All before coming here.

Earlier today, I'd driven a cart down the path I'm standing on. And now, I look down and see my slippered feet at the edge of a crater. The crying woman and the other diéman who are weeping and moaning and shrieking along with her are all in the crater. And the dugulenw who stare dumbly at them are all over on solid ground.

I don't know how much time passes, but eventually a français sees the growing crowd of brown faces. Then another and another. And the horror on their faces turns evil. I get the feeling they're looking straight at me, even as I know they're looking past me. I'm too light to be noticed. My nose too thin, my hair too thin, my brownness too thin.

Then the riot begins.

It's like watching a river overflow during wet season. Formerly peaceful and burbling and harmless, now raging and vengeful and all around you.

I'm safe. Somehow.

The river breaks around me. The occasional shoulder checks me. The occasional outstretched hand claws past, through my face. I lose my cane at some point. But I'm still standing. Right in the middle of the torrent. I think I'm still staring at the cluttered sky. But then I squint past the vicious French people and see the colors of the Kingsguard and, around them, the gendarmes.

They run straight through the crater, not even bothering to glance up at the impossible thing hovering over their heads. I turn just in time to hear the first thud. The first bone-crack.

The crash of bodies raises the shouting and screaming and wailing to a new pitch. It's like thunder all over again. Another explosion. And the whole mass of the city is tangled together.

I don't really know why I don't move, why I can't move. I'm in my body. I can feel everything, hear everything just fine. See it too. But something about a big chunk of the city floating in the air just fixes me in place. And it's like I'm waiting for something. Waiting for the girl who was dying in my apartment late one night to appear among the mess.

I know why I can't move.

I'm still trying to solve a case.

While a riot is going on all around me, while diéman are beating the shit out of dugulenw and while the gendarmes join them and while some of the dugulenw try to fight back, while most flee, I'm trying to solve a case.

The thing that gets me out of my stupor is, of course, a fa-miliar face.

Somewhere in the thick of the scrum, I see him. Moussa. And I'm moving before I can ask my body—tell it—to do otherwise.

At first, I'm behind everybody. I grab one shirt collar, yank the guy back. Grab another. Shove a Frenchwoman to the ground. Pull another by the hair out of my way. They probably all think I've got their bloodlust. Makes it easier to fight my way closer to the center of it all. And that's where it's really turned into a mêlée. Diéman and dugulen duking it out. A gendarme clubbing dugu-lenw two at a time across the face, knocking out teeth indiscrim-inately. Two Frenchmen brawling over who gets to tear apart the fallen dugu boy at their feet. A group of Frenchwomen clawing at a gendarme's outfit in revenge for taking away their prized kill. It's a mess. A damned mess.

And there's Moussa in the middle of his own circle with a baton in his hand, legs spread wide and his arm wrapped around the throat of a dugulen youth. Moussa's lips are peeled back in a rictus snarl. He's glaring. But then I notice the faces surrounding him. They're all white. Moussa's not arresting the boy. He's saving him.

Blood trails from Moussa's mouth and stains his shirt and pants in blotches, along with clumps of dirt and ash.

Moussa's slowly backing his way through the crowd, toward the dugu side. Somehow people make space behind him.

But then someone clubs him on the back of the head. He whirls around, switches the kid to his other arm, and cracks the culprit's skull open. Before another guy can jump on Moussa's back while he's turned, I leap into the fray and tackle the guy out of the way.

Immediately, feet land on me. I curl up, grab a leg and snap it. The folks beating me pause for a moment. They can't see what

I just did but they can hear the blood curdle in their comrade's scream. And that's when I hop up and force my thumbs into the guy's eyes.

A rule of thumb for whenever you're getting jumped. Give up on the idea that you'll ever win. You can't take on four, five, six on your own. What you can do is make an example out of one of them. Pick one, tear him to pieces.

So this time I feel pretty satisfied by the time I get knocked out. Second time today.

CHAPTER FIFTEEN

There's no Temple this time. And I can see out of both eyes. A little bit at first, then more and more. But I want to squint again because the sun's still pretty high in the sky. A figure blocks out the sun. A head. Turns it into eclipse. Then the head kinda perches to one side. Like a bird.

"Hey, kid," I murmur, though my mouth feels like it's been stuffed with cotton.

A small but firm hand lifts me up at the back and suddenly water's flowing down my throat. It's a surprise, so I choke most of that initial mouthful down the front of my shirt. But the urchin clucks and I'm better about the next one.

"How long was I out?"

When my eyes adjust to the shade of the makeshift shelter we're in, I can see the kid crouched on his haunches again right next to me. There's a note of concern in his gaze I never saw before. This kid, always full of surprises. "You're not so old, are you?"

I try to push myself further upright, but it's like someone's kicking my ribs in all over again. "Who told you I was old?" I grimace my way forward but can't make it. So I lie back down and let out a sigh. "Crazy what happened, huh."

Much as I try to chat the kid up, he's strangely silent.

"Where are we? This your home?" The roof looks low. Sunlight comes through spaces in the wood slats. I can't tell if there's any furniture around or any jugs or bowls. Any jewelry or pottery. Anything to make this feel like somewhere someone lives. But you never know with urchins.

"One of them."

"That's right. The city's your home."

"Office."

"What?"

"The city's our office."

"Right." I chuckle. That hurts too. "Is that loan officer here too?"

"I only rescue you."

"Not Moussa?" Out of the corner of my eye, I can see the kid's look. He doesn't ask who Moussa is. Doesn't need to.

He shakes his head. "Just you."

"That's too bad."

The urchin doesn't ask me why I said that. Instead, surprising me, he says, "I saw him try to save that boy. But it was too late. There were too many of them."

The way he says "them" will stick with me for a while, I know that much.

"He's your friend? The policier?"

"How'd you know he was policier?"

"He wasn't holding that baton like he stole it. He was holding it like someone who has held one for a long time. He's beaten many people with it."

"Maybe he's even beaten you with it."

The urchin chuckles. "Maybe."

"Nah, Moussa wouldn't hit a kid. Not like that." I grimace away some new pain at the small of my back. "He's never been that way."

"How do you know him?"

I try to suss out the kid's intentions. What's the question under the question?

Then he says, "Are you policier too?" And I figure it out.

"No," I tell him. "I'm not policier. Not ofisiden ye."

"Not or not anymore."

Clever kid. "I wasn't ever policier. Never worked with the flics. Never wore the tarboush or the stripes. Almost did. Flirted with it. No. I was sorodassi."

The kid grows so still he might as well be furniture. "Soro-dassi." It's a wonder-filled hiss out of his lips.

I force myself upright. Fire in my ribs be damned. Thunder in my head be damned. "That make me a monster to you?"

The kid is looking me in the face, and he's never looked more like a kid than he does in that moment. Like when you're walking into the lake and the bottom goes out from under you and you get a hint—just a hint—of just how deep the water goes. Deep enough to kill you. That's how the kid is looking at me right now. Like I'm the deep of a lake that could choke him dead.

"Hurts me to laugh, kid. I'm not gonna hurt you." I push all the way up into a sitting position. The blanket that was on me falls onto my lap. "Besides. That was a long time ago."

"There were dugulenw in the army?"

I don't know what to tell the kid. It's like his world's been blown up and now he's gotta look at the pieces of his home floating in the air above his head. "You could tell I was dugulen?"

"You're not dugulen." There's new metal in his voice. A hardness like the kind a farmer hits when he tries planting seeds in drought-ridden soil.

"How's that?"

"You hit a français and you're not in the kaso right now."

"Well, I think I got you to thank for that. Saved my life, kid. Remember?"

And now the kid's frowning at me like he might wanna take that back.

"And to be honest," I say under my breath, "I think I hit a couple of 'em." I glance at the kid, and things are still tense for a bit, but then he smirks and that gives us both permission to laugh a little. When the laughing quiets, I reach out—I don't know why—and put my hand on his. "Hey, you wanna talk about it? About . . . well, what happened?"

The urchin looks at me like I've turned into half a giraffe. I guess no one's ever asked him that question before.

"'Cause it's a lot, you know. Seeing that. I'm sure you got questions. Allah knows I got questions, that's for sure. I mean, first of all—"

"How did they get like that?"

And his voice is so small that I almost don't hear it. If it weren't for the fact that there's not a single other thing making noise in our room, I might've missed it.

"It was like the dugu girl. In the square. They were floating just like her."

He doesn't sound scared, but I know that he is. "They were," I say. Quietly.

"It was pretty."

"It was what?"

"Pretty." His eyes are shining and his fingers are jittery now. "Like a rug or a painting."

"People died."

"People die every day. But that . . . that was . . . I hope the others saw it. Maybe I'll show them later if they didn't."

The kid's getting off track and I want to bring him back to the fact that this is serious stuff. Mysterious stuff. Murder-mystery stuff. But sometimes when you're working a case, best to let whoever's on the other side of the table keep talking. Maybe they'll give you something you can use. A bit of pearl hidden in the riverbed.

"I see the way you're looking at me right now. I'm not worried it'll happen to us."

"But it happened to the girl."

"She was . . ."

I think that's it. "Did you know her?"

The kid is cross-legged.

"You know her people?" I can't seem to get away from this girl, no matter how good it is for my soul to leave her behind. I've been haunted before. But hauntings are just unanswered questions. Things left unsaid. The comebacks and the "I love you"s of it all. The quicksand of "why." And I can't tell if getting this kid to talk about her is pulling me out or pulling me back in.

But all of a sudden, the kid's got no more words left.

I flex my fingers, part out of habit, part to try to bring strength back into them. Then I start massaging my thighs, trying to get the blood going again. "Well, then" is all I say to the silence. When I'm confident enough I can stand without collapsing, I struggle to my feet.

"But your cane," the kid says, rising with me, almost like he's ready to help an old man cross the street and not get run over by a carriage.

I wave him away. "Don't need it."

"But you're still hurt. You need to rest."

"Now you're starting to sound like Moussa."

The kid grows quiet. Obviously pondering something deep. "Does he love you?"

The kid didn't ask if I loved him, which woulda been the easier question to answer. Just barely. "I think he does." I have to crouch. The ceiling's about as low as I thought it might be. But I see the opening and how coming out of that will shoot me into an alley. It's quiet in here, but from all the feet I see walking by, we're probably somewhere in the Ethnic Quarter. Maybe not all the way in the Twentieth, but probably not far.

"Where're you gonna go?"

"I gotta go back."

"What if the loan officer's waiting for you?"

"I'll find another cane to beat him away with." I smile. "Thanks, kid. For saving my life."

"I'll do it."

"Do what? You already did it."

"The property records. I'll get them for you."

Which stops me in my tracks. "Now, why would you do that? I'm broke, remember?"

The urchin shrugs. "When you get rich, you pay me before you pay the government."

None of those things are ever gonna happen, but the kid knows it too. So I pat him on the head. "You know Zoe's?"

"The shisha spot?"

"Yeah. When you got the records, meet me there tomorrow."

"Why not tonight?"

"I got a few more errands to run. And, well, last time I was there, some guys didn't quite like it."

"You want me to bring backup."

I chuckle. "You know me, kid. I'll never say no to some backup."

The kid spits in his hand and sticks it out.

I look at it for a second, then spit in my hand, and shake. And I know in my heart that I got no intention whatsoever of walking out on this deal.

CHAPTER SIXTEEN

I'm curious more than anything else.

What's it gonna look like in the lower light? It's been a day. A day and a half really. I've gotten stomped out twice. By dugulenw and français. I've had to question my friendship with Moussa. I may have gotten ripped off by a street kid. And I barely avoided a loan officer. Only thing that got him off my back was the literal end of the world. One of the busier days of my life but not by much.

I was mistaken about where the kid's hideout was. Initially, I thought we were somewhere kind of deep in the Ethnic Quarter. Some part of the market where what happened in the French Quarter was news people barely paid attention to or a whisper dismissed as superstition. Explosion? Probably just an earthquake. You know the river's drying up and have you heard about what Bamako's daughter did? That sort of thing. I thought I'd come out of that hiding place and find myself among a throng of people just minding their own business, maybe heading to the mosque for maghrib while the place flipped over into its nighttime self.

But, no. I'm still, somehow, just outside the French Quarter. I can see the Mize clearly from here.

There's a lot the kid said that I stew on. Looking at the whole mess in the sky as I get closer, I do see something artful about it all. But I dash away that thought quick as it comes. Next, however, is the connection we made between this and the girl floating in the square what feels like a month ago.

I try not to think of the girl in the air like that as something pretty, something aesthetically arranged. But the thought persists. There was a beauty to her in life, brief as I knew her in it. But that got twisted, distorted, chewed up and spat out when her killer left her like they did. You could say the same about the devastated French Quarter. Riding through it on Zanga's cart, it was pretty. Neatly arranged. It was cold and sterile and whatnot, but it was pleasing to look at. No dirt except for where it was meant to be. Cobblestone pathways, hushed conversation, parasols, top hats, vestments in black and white. Looked like something arranged by a god building a park. Then all that arrangement, chewed up and spat out into the sky, so that it all looks like chaos. My eyes go wide in shock.

Like the chaos of the Ethnic Quarter.

I might be making connections where there aren't any. And generally when working a case, the complicated explanation is usually the wrong one. But now I'm out here in the failing sunlight trying to figure out why the diéman who killed the girl would want to do this to their own people.

The possibility that this might be jatigewalekela crosses my mind, but I run into the same problem. If the goal was to attack the French, then why kill one of your own? I'm back to that conversation I had with Oumar. Maybe the war ain't over for some people. I look at the ground under my feet and try to imagine the tunnels the urchin was talking about. A whole web of them right underneath me. Filled with dugulenw smuggling weapons or families, thinking those two are one and the same. Filled with frightened folks. Angry folks. Furious folks. Sad folks. Filled with war preparations. War actions. And the sorodassi none the wiser.

I've been walking this whole time and I'm practically on top of the Mize when I start to notice the commotion all around me. It's hushed, quieter than earlier in the day. But in the shadows cast by the setting sun, gendarmes and ofisiden ye haul dugulenw out of their homes or their offices. A pair will have a slumped dugu scholar between them. Or maybe a dugu woman dressed in scholar robes will walk between them with her head bowed and her hands bound in front of her.

It's a roundup.

Been a while since the dugulenw got hit with mass arrests. They were much more common right after the war, when the jatigewalekela were more obvious. Easier to see. Back when the war wounds were still fresh.

It's a little startling to see them now. I imagine the French thought themselves too civilized to react in this way to being harmed. That indiscriminate lashing out isn't the way to keep what they built glued together. But then I remember how the cops and the military police came charging after those français, and I remember that they weren't coming to restrain their fellows. They were backup. They were all the same, that massive white wave crashing into the rocks. Obliterating them. This? This is just cleanup. That's what somebody somewhere is telling themselves.

And it's tough watching those dugulenw who thought they were assimilated or on their way there being hauled off like that. Dugulenw who had nothing to do with whatever it is that happened, presumably. Dugulenw who thought they were safe, dressed up as they were. Dugulenw who maybe looked up into the sky right after that explosion and saw their own homes floating closer to the clouds than to them. Dugulenw who maybe saw a loved one up there in the mess. A father, a mother, a sibling. A lover. A friend. How far is this gonna set things back?

It's harder to look at the thing in the sky as something pretty when I got all these questions swimming through my head.

But most of the dugulenw getting arrested go without protest. Who knows how long they'll spend in the kaso? A day? A month? They probably don't. The guys arresting them probably don't either. That's how these things go. But they head off nonetheless. They know the deal. Never forgot it. No matter how quiet peacetime has been.

Then I remember a look the kid gave me when I told him I was sorodassi once upon a time. He looked at me like I coulda been one of the gendarmes now "escorting" helpless dugulenw to the dank darkness of a kaso cell. When's the last time he was ever that close to the enemy? That's what being half français makes me. The Enemy.

Deeper into the French Quarter, I start to make a wide circuit and come upon a row of untouched apartments. There's a little bit of sprawl here, but, for the most part, the buildings got that verticality that makes the rest of this part of the city look the way it looked.

Either no dugulenw live in this part or the sweeps in this part have ended. It's quiet enough that either can be true. But I look out on those front porches and there's no broken furniture. No split-in-half wooden desks, no crushed jewelry boxes. No demolished pianos. It's still peaceful here. Like the stuff that happened earlier today is a world away and not around the corner.

No one outside. But not far, I see a shimmering bundle of white out on the sidewalk. It's tiny, looks more like a bundle of cloth than anything else. But it stands out against the growing darkness. The shadows now, I can't tell if it's the sunset or if it's the cataclysm from earlier in the day. But in those shadows stands what I realize is a woman. An older woman. The closer I get, the more wrinkles I see on her face. A wind I don't feel has her white gown whispering about her. She's tiny.

I stop in front of her and follow her gaze. She's looking at it too.

For a long time, we stay like that. From this angle, there's almost no sky to see at all.

"It's not just their bones up there in the sky," she says.

I have my arms folded in front of me. I chance a glance her way. "'Their'?"

She says nothing.

Then I look closer. And I see it. She's got diéman skin and all her features make her look like someone's grand-mère, an elderly, dignified, if occasionally confused française. But I see it. She's a dugulen.

"If they knew what they'd built their home on . . ." But she doesn't finish.

The memory of all those assimilated dugulenw getting hauled off rushes back. I'm angry. "Why choose to live here? With them?"

What she says next, she says with the kindest face, the calmest voice, the gentlest timbre. "There is not a sun bright enough to match my hatred of the français."

"You think they deserved this?"

She closes her eyes and smiles, then slowly shrugs her shoulders. "It does not matter what I think. Allah will as Allah wills. And we each bear our curses as we choose to. My curse is the form I was given. Cut me, and you will find the same blood as fills those bodies in the Ethnic Quarter, the same blood that has flowed in the dugu for as long as it has existed. And yet to look at me is to see one of them. Why do you think Allah did this?"

I ask myself that every time I look in the mirror. "Teach us about our common humanity or some bullshit like that?"

She does that closed-eye chuckle again. "If that were the case, He would make the français look like us."

"Us?"

"You are not a mystery to me."

"You're deux-fois too?"

"No. My blood's purer than yours. But . . . well, my curse."

"Well, why do you live here, then? Why not screw off and spend your life with your people in the souq then?"

She sighs, her eyes open again. Sniffs the air. "The Harmattan hasn't come yet. It is supposed to be the season of dust storms. The sand covers the footprints of what came before. The haze blinds us. It kills our crops. It is supposed to remind us of Who controls all, that each of us is singular and so is our relationship to Allah. Then it passes and we are returned to our loved ones. We are returned to the earth." She faces me. "The français, they are a Harmattan that never ends. I lost my sister to the Harmattan. So, to make her spirit happy, I live among them. I laugh with them. I buy bread with them."

"And your kids?"

"I would never risk having a child that would look like this."

For a long time, we're silent. I'm looking at her. Then I'm looking straight ahead. Seeing nothing.

"Come in. You're shivering. Let me tell you what the français did to my family." When she sees me hesitate, she says, "I'll make tea."

And for some reason, I'm powerless in the face of that.

CHAPTER SEVENTEEN

It's fully nighttime by the time I leave the old lady's place. Maghrib prayer's a memory.

She stands in her doorway, silhouetted by lamplight from her kitchen. She doesn't wave. She smiles. Then she shuts the door. That's the last of the light.

The explosion that day took a bunch of the gaslights with it, so I fumble my way through wreckage and around destruction, trying to retrace my steps. Not get lost.

It's too dark for me to see, but I wonder if anyone else is making the trip. I can't be the only one still out here. This is all enough to scare someone indoors. But imagine being a français and seeing what happened to your neighbors who were indoors when it happened. That idea that nowhere's safe, that brings me back to the whole terrorism thing and for the fifteenth time since my second beating, I'm convinced the jatigewalekela got something to do with this.

As I'm picking my way over bent steel and broken wood and severed park benches and the rubble that was once upon a time a statue, I try to picture what that old lady's dead sister woulda thought about today. When the old lady told me what had happened to her, all I saw was the dead girl's face. They woulda been two generations apart. A war and a half between them. I wanted to tell the old lady times were different now. There was no need to hate the français like that anymore. They can't hurt you like they used to. But then I think of that girl all cut up and hanging in the air like a trophy, and I remember they can still hurt us plenty. Suddenly, it's "us." Maybe that lady's story's working on me more than I thought.

The urge to leave all this behind fills me suddenly. Before I know what I'm doing, I'm running faster than I got any business running. I'd barely woken up from my first beating before I got my second and in between, this attack strikes the city. There's no way I should be upright. On top of that, I can't see where I'm going. No telling what bench or home or pile of rubble I'll stumble over, what crater I'll fall into and break my neck at the bottom of. But I gotta get out of here. Just get out the other end of . . . I still don't know what to call it.

I can't tell when exactly I make it out of the French Quarter, but eventually I do. Not that the noise is different or the quality of the silence. More a change in the air. Bad spirits, they're thinner here. Back there, the air's thick with them. Most days, you feel like you've left the dugu behind with all its superstitions and its ways of worship. Then something happens and you open your eyes to realize you've been mumbling a prayer this whole time. Silly me, thinking I could forget half of me just like that.

The world around me is still all shades of black. An inkier black than what the city usually looks like at night. It's unrecognizable. A part of me thinks that just waiting for my eyes to adjust will make the city legible again. But the handwriting's been dumped in a glass of water. I can't read this place anymore. And it ain't just the lamplights being broken that's done this.

Maybe I've just been up too long.

That's gotta be it. That's why I'm seeing the city now rising up outta the ground like it's the middle of the day. That's why I find myself stopping in front of one brick building and putting my hand to the wall. Running my fingers along the bullet holes, thinking they're pretty. There's a couple dozen of them. They're about eye-height. I try to step around the bodies at my feet that ghost around my legs anyway. I'm hallucinating again.

Staggering forward, I hit a bit of wood and crane my neck up to see the platform the guillotine's balanced on. And I'm looking up, straight up, into the nose hairs of the guys manning the thing, a français reading some proclamation and a dugu officer dressed in a stupid imitation of his master, and my gaze catches the eye of the poor sap whose head is trapped in the device.

When the blade comes down, I don't hear the sound it makes, because I'm turned around by the sound of an explosion. When I settle, I see Oumar's home in flames in front of me. But how did I get here? I was just in the city square a moment ago and just before that the French Quarter.

The city and its parts all switch up around me. Like there's some kid in my head messing around with puzzle pieces, jamming French parts into the dugu, stacking the Mize on top of La Mairie. And shining the brightest lamp in the world on it all. It feels like the explosion has happened inside me, whatever happened in the French Quarter is the same thing happening behind my eyes.

My head's in my hands. I feel myself spinning and swinging down a street. A broad street but then something knocks me on my ass and I find myself looking up into the moonlit face of an ofisiden ye. His knuckles are white around the wood of his spear.

"It's curfew. What are you doing here?"

I look past the ofisiden ye to see the ground floor of the multistory mud and brick building behind him all lit up. Figures move past the windows. Grown men. That can't be right. There's supposed to be a family in there.

"Move away from here or we will be forced to jail you."

"But I . . ." I look at those windows, then look up at the building face I recognize until I get to the top floor. No lamplight on in there, but plenty of movement. Maybe it's too dark for whoever's up there to see the bloodstain that must surely still be under my window. The bloodstain that no rain's come to wash away. "I live here."

"No, you don't."

"What do you mean?" I climb to my feet. My head's back on straight. Or thereabouts.

"These premises have been commandeered by the Kingsguard and the gendarmerie. It will from now until further notice operate as a forward operating base for the government's forces in response to the most recent terrorist attack carried out by local agitators."

Terrorist attack carried out by local agitators, huh? Well, he says it with that royal sort of authority even the lowliest français seem to manage. Easy enough to take it all as truth, which, if it is, is more than I know about the whole thing.

"Sir, move away from here or—"

"But this is my home." It sounds plaintive when it comes out of my mouth. I want it to sound like a joke, but it sounds like me on the verge of tears.

Which works on the ofisiden ye's insides because he relaxes a little. So do the muscles in his face. "You don't have family you could stay with?"

I shrug, try not to cry.

"Is no matter. They will be turning this whole place upside down before long." Now it's the ofisiden ye's turn to look off into the distance, seeing something that isn't there. "They are going to be making so many of these people homeless." He looks back at me. "What do you do when a bug scares you?"

"You stomp on it," I say, and we share a sorrowful smile.

He's younger than Moussa by about two decades, maybe newly appointed. There's still plenty of color underneath his skin. He hasn't started to gray yet. Not like us. Maybe that's youth. Maybe that's not having fought in a war. But then my heart breaks for the kid, because war's about to happen to him and neither he nor the baby fat on his face can see it coming. He thinks he knows the world, knows the order of things. I can't bear to look at him another second.

So I turn on my heel and head deeper into the Twentieth. When the fresh-faced kid tries to wish me well, I just raise my hand and wave as lazily as I can manage. I don't have the energy for much else.

There's no urgency to my shuffling. I'm the only one out making sounds, odd enough. You'd think even with the curfew that some part of the Ethnic Quarter would still be jumping. Our world isn't theirs, is what the dugulenw frying fish or playing mancala or thieving from each other and chasing each other up and down the street would say. And they'd figure out a way to dodge the ofisiden ye, frustrate the policiers, confound the gendarmes. But there's no one. It's just me. Getting lost in the maze of home.

I contemplate stopping by Zoe's, but I don't wanna take the chance that the government's colonized that place too. I couldn't bear to look at it if that were the case.

Instead, I head into the next alley I find, barely able to fit me sideways and standing. But I shuffle down and manage to curl in on myself, making a pillow of my hands.

"Hey, you," I say to the girl waiting for me in my dreams while I sleep on the street.

CHAPTER EIGHTEEN

I can tell I smell bad because when I wake up, there's a skeleton of a guy holding a water jug out at me. My nose ain't all the way healed yet, so I'm spared both our odors. But I still look at him and want to ask if he's kidding me. But, no. The look on his face is serious. And impatient. So I peel myself off the street, take his jug out deeper into the alley, and wash up real quick. I don't have a change of clothes—the gendarmes probably threw all three of my outfits on the street—so I'm stuck with this djellaba that still has dried blood and bootprints on it. It was either wash myself or wash it. The sans-domicile-fixe didn't have enough water for both.

Still, when I'm done, I dress, hand back the jug, and nod my thanks.

Out in the bustling street, the light of a new day hits hard enough to make me almost forget everything that happened yesterday. Looking around me, the Ethnic Quarter's just as I remember it. I strain my ears, try to pick out bits of conversation. But nobody's talking about it. No mention of the French Quarter, the explosion, whether or not all those homes are still in the sky. No mention of the roundups or the gendarmes and Kingsguard surely on patrol within shouting distance of here.

Some of that's infected me too. My brain isn't as foggy as it was last night. No more hallucinations. Nothing but life around me. I doubt anyone's even stepped on a water bug yet today.

And I've got my sense of mission back. Figure out what the hell is going on in this town.

I don't want to go back to the French Quarter and pick it over for clues. The place is still too thick with noise. Not the type of noise you hear. The type of noise that fills up your head from the inside. Makes it difficult to see. Difficult to find your way through things. Difficult to think. No. Instead, I head to the hospital. But I'm barely halfway there before I hit a roadblock.

This one's different from the roadblocks I've seen in the past. This one's guarded by black-suited gendarmes. The ones with helmets and swords. Not a single ofisiden ye in sight. No spears, no machetes. Nothing but straight lines here.

Nobody tries to get through either. Like they've got the whole Ethnic Quarter closed off. No foodsellers heading into the square. No one servicing French customers. Not today. Maybe not ever again.

Not even worth it to try getting by. Those gendarmes stand like statues. They don't even joke like proper checkpoint guards. I wonder how they deal with boredom, then it occurs to me that I'd never ask a gun or a sword how it dealt with boredom.

My plan was to see if I could suss out anything from French patients getting treated. Somewhere among the wounded, there might be a bit of information. Not an answer to any of the big questions doing the mosquito dance around my head. But something to point me in a direction. Shine a little bit of lamplight on where I'm supposed to go. Knowing if I should go after someone French or someone dugu is different from knowing one of them did it. One of those is a little more my size than the other.

It's not looking like I'll get to the French hospital any time soon. But that doesn't mean the plan's dead. Maybe, just maybe, there are folks being treated in the Temple. I don't know a single français that'd choose to get treated by dugulen hands. But sometimes you fall out of the sky and your house is still up there, and choice ain't something you can reach anymore.

Before I even get there, I see my luck's starting to turn.

The place is overflowing with injured. Bandaged patients ushered every which way by dugulenw nurses, surgeons with patients on beds cauterizing and repairing wounds out in the open, assistants scurrying back and forth with buckets of sanitizing water.

Most of the diéman I see are too preoccupied by pain or trying to stay alive to protest. But a few struggle. A delirious française tries to attack her doctors while half her right leg is missing. Nurses try to hold down another français who thrashes while a masked dugu doctor has scissors and a tiny wooden spoon to his neck, trying to remove a piece of shrapnel.

A lot of the patients look like they came out of the attack. Either they dropped out of the sky or they were caught in the radius, blown outward maybe. The staff outside the hospital are too busy to notice me walking into the open-air stone building. It's got plenty of windows and wall openings and it's got high ceilings to allow for ventilation. Though that means having pots filled with hot stones and coals nearby to heat patients in the cold seasons and to heat tools for operations I don't have the stomach to think about right now. I overhear some of the doctors and assistants, at various points, thank God that this happened during Harmattan season. They call the air that sometimes blows fierce over the land the "doctor wind." Praise it for being so dry and not humid and heavy like during the wet season. Keeps infections low.

The deeper I get in the Temple, I start to realize something. It's segregated. There's no curtain driving a line between the two major parts of the main theater. But you can see it plain as literal day and night. Diéman out front, the first to get treatment from whoever's available. From one angle, it makes sense as their wounds are the most grievous, you'd think. Amputations, emotional damage, all that immediate trauma from the horror some of them still think they're in the midst of. People still crying out that they're stuck in the sky or that the explosion's happening over and over to them, they got that urgency about them. But then in the back are the dugulenw.

First glance, they look like they're in better shape overall. Fewer missing limbs, fewer fevered calls out to missing or dead loved ones. But then I notice just what it is that brought them here.

Contusions, bloody faces, bruises, broken bones. They bear it all quietly. These weren't wounds from the attack. They got these in the riot.

It slows me down, watching all this while I walk. The whispers here from the doctors and nurses, the healers, they're all hushed. Quiet. Conspiratorial, but the conspiracy is just them saying "I understand your pain and your grieving, we are the same color, and you can trust me." That kind of thing.

I wonder if anyone in the diéman side of the Temple would recognize anyone on this side. "Hey, this is the person I kicked in the head" or "this is the boy I wanted to tear apart but gendarmes stopped me" or "that one clocked me good across the jaw but, boy, did I pay him back." Or maybe they blacked out. Happens sometimes during riots, you just forget yourself. Saw it a couple times during the war when things became more close-quarters. You'd see the animal in someone come out. And you'd remember all over again what it looks like for someone to hate someone else. There it is, lurking under the petticoats and the French collars. Most diéman don't have the time or energy to hate someone else, but when they get the chance, they go all in. Not all of them. But enough of them that things are the way they are right now.

About fifty paces away, toward the far back, a physician's

hunched over a woman lying flat on her back. Otherwise unremarkable, except for something I have to squint to notice. Where his hands are. Then I notice how secretive it all feels over there. They're in plain light, but it feels like they're shrouded in shadows. Feels like they're up to something they shouldn't be up to.

I walk faster. But that gives me away.

The surgeon hears me coming, looks up, and doesn't even bother to clean his blood-covered hands before hurrying off.

I rush now, careful not to knock into any doctors or disrupt any of the care work going on, but I stop at the patient for a second.

She's got short hair, cut to make her look like a boy. Her chest is wrapped too. Shirt cut open to reveal the soiled bandages. They don't look like they're covering any wounds and that confirms what I was thinking. She was disguised whenever whatever happened to her happened. Her whole body's covered in sweat and her forehead glows fever red. But the thing that almost freezes me completely is the compact over the left side of her stomach. It looks like it was hastily put together. The bloodstain's still spreading on it. That's where the physician's hands were. On her stomach. In her stomach. Right where the girl's hands had been when she stumbled into my apartment.

The back exit the doctor went through isn't hard to find. But it spits me out onto a back alley that looks like a million others I've walked through. Laundry flaps in the breeze above my head.

But I can smell the cleaning fluid on the air. That gives me all I need.

I head deeper into the alley, crosshatched with light and shadow from the sun coming through and around the buildings. And there's a bit of quiet that I hit that makes me worry for more than a second if I've been lured into a trap. I'm not back at 100 percent, but I can make anyone who comes at me regret it. That cane woulda been nice, though.

A whisper of a white coat around a corner.

I dash after it. Already, in my head, I'm coming up with all the questions I got for the good doctor. Like what was wrong with that girl's stomach? Does he know why she was disguising herself? Was he taking something out of her or putting something in? That last one turns my stomach a little, but it might be the most important one.

I gotta find him.

CHAPTER NINETEEN

The alleys get even twistier and smaller, so small they're only meant for urchins if anyone at all. How the hell did the doctor get through here?

I've lost the scent of antiseptic. Dammit.

Nothing left but for me to get out of this maze, then. So I squeeze as much as I'm able to, at one point getting so stuck that I have to double back. But then I catch the dull roar of a crowd. Right now, I'm so thirsty for sunlight and wide-open spaces that I've got no choice but to follow. A few more minutes of shimmying and catching my breath and climbing over debris blocking my path and I get to the mouth of an alley.

It's so choked with people that I have to shove my way through to what turns out to be a massive open space. Sort of like the square in the city center. Only, this is on the other end of the Ethnic Quarter, out toward the encampments. It looks like sparse unbuilt space, but it's so filled with people that I'm having a harder time breathing here than I did in the back alleys.

I go to double back but then I see it. A puff of black hair with gray at the temples. Attached to a neck that vanishes in a white, blood-dotted doctor's robe. There he is.

Shoulders and arms close in on me. I can't shout that I'm ofisiden ye or that I'm a policier, because that would raise too many questions and still wouldn't get people out of my way fast enough. It'd also be a lie. No, trying to clear a path that way would be too simple and too chaotic. Best I can do is try to use the scrum to my advantage. Sneak up on the guy.

The pointed chatter around me also helps me disguise myself. Makes it look like I'm just a latecomer trying to get to the front.

And that helps me for a bit. But then the doctor glances over his shoulder, and I don't duck in time. His eyes go wide, then he whips his head back around. He's gone.

It's almost like the crowd's gotten thicker. I have to be a bit more violent with the elbows and shoulders. When other people's elbows and hands talk back, they do it loudly. But I try to let it all push me forward. In the back of my mind, though, I'm asking myself what so many people are doing here. Nobody's selling anything, except for maybe a few kid hawkers on the outskirts of the crowd with their wares attached to strings around their necks—bananas and bracelets, that kind of thing. But it's people spread as far as the eye can see. You can't fit a cart in here. There's no fight going on, no pit around which spectators are ogling. Can't smell any meat cooking, so this isn't some sort of party, and there's only soft drumming going on up at the front. Nobody's singing along, so it ain't a concert either.

Maybe gendarmes cornered people here. It looks like this place has the whole Ethnic Quarter squeezed into it. If you wanted to do violence to that part of the city's population, corralling them all into a single space like cattle would be a good way to start. But I don't want to shout a warning cry just yet. These people are smart and they know what a raid looks like. A mass killing, maybe not. But something tells me this ain't that.

Another problem with this crowd, though, is that the body odor swallows up the doctor's scent. So I got nothing to go by except blind luck. Maybe the day's not gonna turn out the way I wanted.

Then I get pushed more toward the front with the shifting of bodies and come to a hard stop when a metal railing hits my stomach. Feels like someone swung it at me. But when I catch my breath, I raise myself a little and see that it's a barrier. And in front of me across a short distance is a raised dais. At the front corners of the square are the drummers and there's a line of them right in front of me too, staring straight ahead while the folks around me belt out a song I haven't heard since I was a kid. Something old and from the dugu. Sounds like the kind of song that existed before this city even went up. The kinda song that old lady in the French Quarter might've sung if she ever had dugulenw kids to sing it to. Maybe the kind of song her mother sang to her when she was that age.

Then it all stops.

A figure has mounted the stage and every sound that ever existed in this square has ended. Cut off at the head. I don't even hear the wind whistling. Whoever this guy is, he's wearing the cleanest sand-colored grand boubou I've ever seen. There's a hint of silver embroidery running vertically in patterns down the torso but a lot of it has been swallowed up by the sleeves of the overgown. Still, it gives the man the look of something celestial. The way light just careens off those stripes. His aso òkè hat has its flap over the left ear. The way it looks, you'd think this is where the French got the idea for berets from. When were we not first at something?

Usually, a guy wears a grand boubou like that, he's got that chin-raise going on. He's got his shoulders back, his chest out. Looks like he owns every piece of land he puts his foot on. But this guy's shoulders are kind of hunched. His chin's angled back toward his chest. And though he's on the bigger end, maybe even has a belly under all of that cloth, he looks shrunken. He looks . . . nervous.

But everybody here, I realize, is waiting for him.

He shakes one shoulder to adjust a sleeve. Then the next. Like he's uncomfortable. Then he clears his throat. His voice, when the first words come out, sounds reedy. Like a bird. An old bird with about three months left to live.

"I want to thank you all for coming out to here this afternoon. I know many of you are working and have left your stalls, your places of business, to stand here today. I know many more of you are out of work or unable to work and have left the shelters you have made for yourselves to come here. And for that, I thank you."

As much as I'm able, I turn around to see how far back the crowd stretches. I can't see the horizon. Can anybody back there even hear this guy?

But he keeps going like that's not a problem.

"For the youth here today, for those too young to remember war and massacres, it may feel like things have always been this way. That the boot has always been on your neck. That milk is difficult to come by. That there are entire swaths of this city you are forbidden from entering. That law enforcement and the king's authorities can single you out and beat you with impunity. When this is all you know, it is easy to believe it has always been this way. It is gravity. It is the movement of the sun and the moon. It is an eternal season, and who can war with the planet's humming? I do not say this as condemnation. I do not condemn the young for their youth. I do not damn them for it. And I ask that you parents, you grandparents, not do the same. They have eyes to see and ears to hear and noses to smell the world around them. The order that has been built up around them. Nor do I condemn my age-mates. I am not young, so I imagine that I share a generation with more than a few of you. You need not confess your ages to me." Chuckles rumble like waves through the crowd. They seem to go on forever, reaching all the way to the back. He's not speaking any louder, but they're all hanging on his every word. Then he turns his gaze on me. "I do not condemn my generation for the world we have left to our young. But I will say that we were not powerless in its construction. We are not blameless. Nor are we wholly without power now. We carry inside each of us a memory of the past. Inside each of our hearts beats an entire history. Joined together, our hearts carry the history of this land, what it was before it became"—he waves behind him to indicate the faraway city center—"this. Our home is what we have envisioned as our home. We are each of us authentically dugulenw. And just as our past resides in our present, so does our future reside in us. So does our future live in us. And it is something which we should face with both of our eyes. Do not shy from this upcoming election. Because if I win, you will see a proper Truth and Reconciliation Commission formed to tell your truths. To tell the truths of what was done to you. What was done to us. By their armies. Elect me and you will see a full accounting of the atrocities these people have sought to paper over with their trees and their apartments and their gated communities. The atrocities many of you bear on your cheeks and in the bruises on your faces this very moment." He narrows his eyes at me. "Elect me and we shall point this place toward a future of our own making, not one imposed on us by others, but one built with our hands and that feeds our stomachs. That soothes our wounds. That protects us from those who would wound us." Now, he redirects his gaze to the crowd. "Elect me, and you shall be electing us. All of us. Thank you for your time."

The whole place erupts. More clapping and stomping and shouting than I've ever heard in my life. Like a continuous peal of thunder. I feel it shuddering every bone of my body.

The guy looks out over the crowd again, smiling, and I get a glimpse of it. The thing that must draw people to him. It's a power, a glow, that makes him seem more than man. Maybe that's just the embroidery.

But even as he turns around and walks back down the stage, I can't but feel like he's still looking at me. That, even as he looked out over the crowd, the only person he saw . . . was me.

The crowd is jubilation and joyful tears behind me, people fainting, practically calling out for the guy to throw his underwear at them. But something tugs my pant leg.

I go to swat the person away when I see it's none other than the urchin.

Proudly holding several pieces of parchment rolled up in a single scroll.

"We can discuss payment later," he says, grinning.

I could kiss the kid.

CHAPTER TWENTY

"Easy! You'll spill my tea!"

I know I should be careful, the way I've got these documents spread on our chipped wooden table, half of them hanging over the side, but I can't help myself. "I'll buy you another one."

"Another pot?!" I can feel his eyes go wide, that's how big they get. "Oh, so you're made of money now?"

"Lady here knows me," I tell him without looking up. "I got a tab." He don't need to know that I ain't paid in a year and a half and Fatouma would walk me to the guillotine herself if she caught me guzzling mint tea in her establishment again.

"I thought you were bringing me to smoke shisha."

"I got a debt to settle there too."

He knocks back another glass, then refills from the pot. The pot was holding down the corner of a map, and as soon as the urchin lifts the pot, the map slides to the ground. I catch it just in time and shake some renegade drops of tea from it, then settle it on top of the others.

The documents are a mess of incomplete information and too much info at the same time. Pages from ledgers recording payments to the central land authority. A partial list of alphabetized homeowners in the French Quarter. A map with the Ethnic Quarter blotted out in diagonal lines. A map with sketches of land outside the outer arrondissements with numbers marked on them. Pages from a French novel about a marquis with a small dick. It's a mess, but I can't blame the kid. I never told him what exactly I was looking for. Hell, I barely knew myself. If pressed, I couldn't say where exactly that warehouse Zanga's boys brought me to really was. Just that it was out in the hinterlands past the French Quarter. Might not even be documented on any map the French have put together yet. But, poring over the ledger pages, I still take the time to tell the kid, "You know, you did real good. This is helpful."

"Really? I just took whatever."

"Nah, you got a good eye for this sort of thing."

The urchin puffs out his chest. "You know, this business runs on customer satisfaction. We stake our reputation on it. No reputable thief in this city leaves behind a trail of unsatisfied customers."

"Sounds a bit like something I would say."

He finishes pouring, then cups his glass in both hands and leans forward. "Oh, yeah?" A dramatic pause. "Well, what exactly do you do? Mister No-Money?"

I'm starting to get the numbering down. Cross-referencing some of the info in these different documents, I can tell now that some numbers are for religious buildings and others for schools. Ah! They're building codes! I flip back to the ledgers. The numbers next to those names. They're not prices or payments. They're codes for the different buildings under the person's ownership. "I'm a chercher," I tell the kid.

"Wait! You're a chercher?" Then he calms. "How come I've never heard of you, then?"

"Why would you have heard of m—" I don't finish the question. I realize what he's asking. He's an urchin. He's probably seen quite a few people in his life vanish. His class of folks, the type of people who live underfoot, they vanish almost as quickly as they show up. One day, a new person stumbles upon your hovel and they've got no family or at least no family they wanna claim. They join your crew or they become someone you care for. Then one day they're gone. Maybe you find them later strung out on khat in a back alley. Or they've been snatched up by ofisiden ye and are passing their days unknown and unclaimed in a kaso cell. Maybe their body turns up later all kinds of ruined and you know, because they are who they are and because you are who you are, that the only questions you can ask are the ones that'll never get answered. "I wasn't very good," I lie.

"So you got better?"

"So I went out of business."

The urchin laughs, but the wind's out of his sails a little bit.

I'm still hopped up on my discovery, so all my attention returns to the numbers next to these names. I've cracked the code a little bit. But now I need to figure out what's the building code for storage facilities. For warehouses.

"Hey!"

I look up and all of a sudden the kid's head is touching mine. He casts a shadow over the papers, but then his finger lands with a thud on a name in the ledger.

"I know that name!"

I move my hand and see what he's pointing at. "Honoré Mirbeau de L'Isle-Adam," I whisper.

"Yeah, that one! I've seen it before."

"Where?"

"L'Isle-Adam! It's all over my old neighborhood. Where Bamuso says we're from. She and Fa used to take me for walks there."

"Where is it?" I shuffle the papers. "Point to it on this map. Here."

His eyes scour the sheet, back and forth, up and down.

"Here, look. This is the Ethnic Quarter." I point, then I point to a different spot. "French Quarter's here. And that's the Mairie.

Centre-Ville's here. And these over here are the outer arrondisse-ments. Now where've you seen L'Isle-Adam?"

He frowns. Squints. "There." He points to an unmarked place beyond the outer arrondissements.

"Wait. Are you sure? How do you know?"

"Bamuso said we weren't from the city. Moved when I was young because the land went bad and the water was no longer good to drink or bathe in. I was too little to remember. But I know that spot's where we're from."

I look closer and I see, faintly, the building codes for residen-tial housing. That doesn't make any sense. Why would a français build apartments all the way out there on the opposite side of the city from the French Quarter? And Adam Island seems like a weird name for a housing development. But it's recognizably French. "You ever been back?"

"What?"

"Since your family moved to the city." I know better than to ask about why he only refers to his parents in the past tense. "You ever go back to look?"

The urchin's expression darkens and he looks away.

I snap my fingers at a server. "Hey, could we get another pot?" Least I can do for dragging the kid through bad memories.

The server whisks himself away, then is back a few moments later with another pot for us, takes the one we drained away. Every time he comes and leaves, he carries a bit of ambient conversa-tion about him. And it's all people gushing about the presidential-candidate guy from the rally. Remembering the way he looked at me chills me, so I shake away the vision like a dog straight out of a river.

"Hey, kid," I ask him, still puzzling over the Adam Island de-velopments. I pause, because I feel bad for what I'm about to do to the kid. But he might be my ticket into a part of this mystery

I haven't been able to crack yet. "You ever see a français walking through the Ethnic Quarter? A diéman?" And I wait.

"Why?" Which was not the response I was expecting.

I raise my head and look him in the eye. Gotta be careful about how I approach this. "You know about what's jumpin' in the Ethnic Quarter. You ever hear about anybody turning up with stomach wounds?"

"Stomach wounds?"

"Yeah. Bodies that look like they've been cut open right here." And I point an imaginary line across the side of my belly, right where the girl had been bleeding what seems like a lifetime ago.

The urchin's frown deepens. "Why are you asking me these two questions?" He leans back, folds his arms across his chest. "Diéman kill us all the time. Even when we don't leave the Ethnic Quarter."

"There's a difference between diéman getting you killed and diéman killing you."

He shrugs, and some of that standoffishness slides off of his shoulders. "I mean, I've stolen drugs for them when they come sneaking through the souq, thinking they're slick. Heck, I've stolen drugs from them too. But everything they carry is always shit. You think a diéman's killing us and cutting us open?"

Not necessarily in that order, I wanna tell him. But I keep my mouth shut.

His eyes go wide. "Does it have to do with Adam Island? But why would a rich man kill us and defile our bodies?"

Now it's my turn to shrug. Because they can, I wanna tell him. But I keep my mouth shut.

"There was talk of . . ."

"Talk of what?"

"Well." He leans in. "That girl in the city square? The one floating in the air like all those buildings in the French Quarter?"

"Yeah?"

"That wasn't the first time we seen that."

I try not to look too hungry, but I'm practically champing at the bit.

"But we don't talk about it."

"Don't talk about it, why? Who's trying to cover it up?"

"If they find out I talked to you about it, they'll kill me and my crew."

"I thought nobody knows this city better than you. Can't you escape or something? Hide out?"

"They have eyes everywhere."

"Who?"

But the kid's shut down. He's not gonna give me anymore.

I let out a sigh and start rolling up the scrolls.

"Where are you going?"

"You're gonna show me your old home. Now, hurry, before the servers notice we're gone."

CHAPTER TWENTY-ONE

I have to say, it feels good having a partner. Although, I'd never call him that. Don't want the kid getting any big ideas.

But our little get-together at the teahouse gives me hope. Or at least a sense of gratitude. Luck, fortune, the hands twirling the stars around in the sky, maybe they don't all got it out for me. Finding the kid when I did, when it seemed like I'd run up against a mud wall in this investigation, has been nothing if not fortuitous.

I have to keep remembering that he's still just a kid, though. He's seen plenty. Even if he didn't fight in the war, he could go pound-for-pound with any haunted-eyed vet for horrors witnessed. I'm pretty sure. And sometimes you gotta remember that kids, they don't got the stamina for seeing brutalities and savageries that you do. Can't just plow forward in the face of monstrosity like you. Staring into the abyss, their eyes dry out quicker than yours. So this might mean having to take things a little slower, which I get. Means I'll have to hold back on pushing him for more on the murders. The Floaters. But he did me a solid back there. Didn't have to spell it out, but he confirmed my theory: all the Floaters, they had stomach wounds. Just like the girl in the city square.

I wonder if Moussa's got that little bit of info. If the coroners have had time to get back to him on that. Then I remember that they've probably got a couple dozen wagonloads of new bodies to go through and catalog and maybe quite a few of them are français so meanwhile the dugulenw with the clues cut into them gotta go decay past usefulness.

Guilt pinches my heart. That's maybe the first time I've thought of Moussa since I last saw him. Since we were both getting the shit kicked out of us by français. First time I've thought of Moussa since I'd tried to save his life.

The souq's got its color all the way back. You'd forget there were still barricades manned by gendarmes sealing the Ethnic Quarter off from the rest of the city. My guess is it all comes down to that one guy and that one speech. If I were to just look at his words or hear them from someone else's mouth, I wouldn't give them a second thought. Just some delusional fool or some troublemaker with a business eye for local grievance. Looking to monetize being oppressed. But that's not what he looked like talkin' to all those people. They believed him. They still do. That's all the hum and buzz around me. People living their lives with an eye toward the future. It's filling the whole place with an energy I'm not used to. Like we got a new, different season on the calendar. Something different from the wet season and the Harmattan. Not knowing what that new season'll look and feel like unnerves me.

As we walk, I try to shoot glances into storefronts or around street corners, anywhere I might catch a glimpse of a random diéman still trying to sample dugu wares. That's how it is for them a lot of the time. The transgression, that's the spice on the tagine that gives it the perfect flavor. The person you're not supposed to screw, the shisha you're not supposed to smoke, the arak you're not supposed to drink. The lips you're not supposed to kiss. Throw up a few barricades and marble-faced, sword-toting gendarmes, and the loins start to stir. But even with all that temptation, I don't spot a single diéman. If the kid sees any, he doesn't say anything. Just moves along with a little bit of hurry in his step. He's not rushing us anywhere, but he's got a destination in mind. He's so at ease that I cast my gaze at the rooftops flanking us to see if I'll catch any pairs of eyes looking down on us. Crew members making sure their leader's safe. All this talk of a crew, of his family of fellow urchins, fellow thieves, and I don't think I've seen a single one. Kid could be lying, of course. Wouldn't put it past him. Which would make him a hell of a salesperson. But them other kids could just be that good at staying hidden. The thought of all those little ankle-kickers spread like army units throughout the Quarter, in all the perfect cubbies and slices between buildings, ready to leap out and do battle at a moment's notice, that image puts a smile on my face.

"What'd you think of the guy's speech?"

"Oh, the Murutilen? You know that's what they call him, right? Murutilen?"

I chuckle. The Rebellious One. "For a rebel, he seems kinda . . . I dunno, soft-spoken?"

"If he gets the ofisiden ye off our backs, I'm not complaining." The kid threads his fingers behind his head while he walks, elbows all poking out. Not a care in the world. "He's the only one doing this whole election thing not talking about kicking the French out."

"Isn't that what people want?"

He whirls around, offended. "Are you nuts? The français are fantastic for business. Why would I steal for people who already know where to find what they're looking for? Besides, there's no easier mark in the world. Them? They don't even know what they want half the time, they just show up here all googly-eyed and drooling. So you get to tell them what they want and convince them they've been looking for it their whole lives. Try that with any uncle or auntie in the souq and see if they don't break a whole maraq over your head."

The kid is good for a laugh, I'll give him that. Another good thing about having a partner. Comic relief. You spend so much of the job looking the worst of what we do to each other in the face, you get to feeling like you're drowning without even realizing how deep in danger you are. Then out of nowhere, through the water, splashes a hand pulling you back to the surface. Breath of fresh air is what this kid is.

Just as the Ethnic Quarter starts to thin out and the streets get wider and there's more space for kids to play football in, I start to see the beginnings of it. Don't know how I could have ever missed it. They're not doing anything to hide.

Two whole rows of Colonial apartments going up just past the hill we stand on. A river burbles like a crystal-blue knife scar through the settlement. They've even built a curved wooden bridge over it.

"Before, they were all the way there." The urchin points far off in the distance to the base of nearby ridges. "All of this is new."

It's like what the French Quarter mighta looked like in the womb. No sprawling parks yet, but there are partially cobblestoned sidewalks instead of dirt paths. Like the sand started getting leprosy. The skinny trees with their neatly pruned bushes are spread farther out. Some of them still got their roots in sacks next to holes that haven't been dug yet. Red dust blows over the whole scene. But the white on the houses, the white of their walls, comes away untouched. And I don't know why, but that's stranger to me than people floating in the air with their guts cut out.

They don't belong here. They're . . . they're foreign. The sand can't stand to touch them.

What's gotten into me?

I want to go back to how I was before. Before I saw this. Before I cared about all of this. Before, when any time dugulenw and français met, it was some individual tragedy or miracle I only got to pay witness to. Back to when they were all just cases to solve. This . . . this is different. This is bigger. All of sudden, it's all bigger somehow. And I can't for the life of me figure out when it stopped being about a girl who showed up in my apartment asking me to hide her.

A sign waves in the breeze, a flapping piece of banner held by two stakes on opposite sides of the river. Between us and the settlement. And out toward us reads the sign: L'ISLE-ADAM.

Just a faded number on a piece of parchment rolled up under my arm, but here it is in front of me now.

"And where did your family live?" It's a struggle to get the words out.

The kid looks at me for a long time, probably trying to figure out what it is that's happening behind my face right now, whatever it is that's got me trembling with fury. Then he points a little past the bridge at where a tall multi-unit apartment building stands. "There."

A young diéman steps out onto the cobblestones, stumbles out, really. But when he looks back up at the opened doorway, he smiles. Beatifically. And a française pokes her head out, lace bonnet and everything, and blows him a kiss and says something we got no chance of hearing all the way up here.

And that's what does it.

I'm gonna kill him for this.

CHAPTER TWENTY-TWO

They don't see me coming. None of them do. Least of all Zanga.

I'm a Harmattan barreling through the entrance to Zoe's, swirling dust and coal sparks in the air around me. Bounding up the stairs three at a time, practically yanking the railing out of place. And there's a moment when I get to the second floor and see Zanga all spread out over the far cushions with his goons lounged around him where I pause. My shoulders heave. I feel like I've got claws. I can hear the growl rumble in my throat. Then I see red.

I'm at least two swings in before I realize I've even ripped a two-by-four from the upstairs railing. But blood flings and splashes from its end. That just drives me crazier. I slam it down twice more, three times, four. In the haze, I only catch snatches of shouting:

—gonna kill you! Don't move—
—race-traitor—
—how's it feel, huh?—
—jump me? Jump me?!—
—diéman-loving, white-faced souroukou—
—rat bastard—
—bleeding—
—split your shit-ass wuulo skull—
—wide—
—open—

The crack-thuds get wetter. The hands clawing at my face, the hands I swat away and work my way around, they get slower. Lazier. More limp. Then I snap out of it.

I'm straddling Zanga. The heaviest silence in the world sits on my shoulders. I've never heard anything like it, except maybe on the battlefield. But even then, you could hear the smoke hissing from the ground or the faraway moaning of the dying. Even if the horrible thing you'd done filled the air with enough soundless horror to choke the breath from your lungs, there was still at least some noise to latch on to. There was at least the thump of your own heartbeat. But this time around, I don't even hear that. There's just everyone surrounding me, slack-jawed while I have this wooden beam raised above my head, ready to kill the man sneering up at me through bloody teeth.

Then I begin to hear my breathing. How it grumbles in the back of my throat. Scrapes and rattles back there. Sweat slipping from my eyelids, my chin, plopping on the floorboards, thudding into the rug.

Zanga's sneer deepens, even as blood covers his face. "You're a big man, eh?" he hisses, low enough so that only I hear it. "Go on. Do it." He moves his head to the side and spits out a glob of blood. It clears his mouth. "Swing that beam. Kill a dugulen. You know you want to. I'm the race-traitor? Go ahead. Murder me, tubabu."

I lean in. I don't feel sorry for what I've done to him. I'm still bubbled up with menace. "Maybe I will. And your français partner? The guy you're colluding with to displace your own? Maybe he'll have to find some other dugulen tiga head to clear the dugu so young, pretty diéman can move in and take over."

"Colluding with the French? That's rich coming from a war criminal."

Like a knife ripping up my spine. I'm on fire. "I'm not gonna kill you." I raise my arm and torque. "I'm just gonna cripple you."

"You'll do no such thing."

I look up. All the air in the upper room switches. Everyone's gaze like gravity goes to the far end of the room by the stairs. The steps are slow. Deliberate. They come in threes. A click, a shuffle, another shuffle. They take their time, those steps.

Eventually, we all see the top of a hijab poking up over the upper level's floor. Then the rest of her head, covered by a cloth so blue it's black. The robe is shapeless around her. She looks like a pillar with waves undulating through her. She pauses at the top of the stairs. To catch her breath? To prepare herself for what she's about to see? Match it with what she imagined from the sounds she's heard? Is she gathering the spirits around her?

It feels like that last one is the right question. Because when Zoe turns her amber eyes on us, we're frozen in place. Turned into splashes of paint on a canvas. Or threads in a rug. None of us can move. None of us dare.

Her gaze roves the scene, lingers for a moment on the faces of each of Zanga's goons, settles on me, dips to the upside-down, broken face of her son, then comes back up to me. Now is when the shame hits. Hard enough to nearly knock me over.

Nobody speaks.

Until Zoe claps her lips and says, "Let him up."

I obey instantly.

"You've gotten blood on my rugs."

The bloodied beam of wood plummets from my hand. "Auntie, I'm sorr—"

She puts up her free hand, the one not holding her cane. And it's like walking into a wall.

Zanga pushes himself over and comes up to his hands and knees. He coughs a little more blood on the floor, then smears his forearm across his nose and mouth. It comes back crimson. Then he gets to one knee, then is standing again.

He's got his back to me. He doesn't turn all the way, but turns to look at me out the corner of his eye over his shoulder. Just a glance, but I know what it means. It's a test. Will I buckle here? Was this just a temporary thing? Me feeling myself in the moment but willing to take a beating later? Or is this something else? Is it me willing to kill him if I need to? Is it me not being afraid of the français in me? Not being afraid to wield it for the weapon it is when the situation demands? The next moment, he's hobbling toward his bamuso, who doesn't even look him in the eye. She doesn't make a move, but we all know he's been dismissed.

That leaves me and the person whose rug I got blood on. And all of Zanga's goons arranged in various postures of deference behind me.

"How are you, Boubacar?" she asks me. Her expression hasn't changed. There isn't a trace of a smile on her face. The undisturbed river of threat in her voice is my only clue as to how she feels right now.

"I . . . I'm fine, Zoe."

"Fine? I don't think that word means what you think it means." She doesn't take a single step closer to me. Hasn't indicated she wants me to get closer to her either. "Is there something you want to say to me?"

"S . . . sorry?"

A ghost of a smirk at the edge of her lips. Then it's gone. "Take a seat."

It's like her words are physical hands pushing me back and onto the cushions. Slowly, stately, she gathers her robe and sits down beside me but at a small distance. Like I got something she doesn't want to get on her.

"How's the business?"

"The . . ."

"The people finding. Slow going, I imagine."

"Wh . . . how . . ."

"Don't be daft, Boubacar. I know you haven't had work in months at the very least. I know you worry about it constantly. And I know you've thrown yourself in the middle of a matter far too big for you because you think it's the only thing that can cure your itch."

"Cure my itch." That last sounds meaner than I want it to sound.

"You're in too deep. And you've lost yourself. That is the only explanation I can think of for why you would think you had permission to do all of this in my place of business." With a light wave, she indicates the mess on the floor, the broken railing, the bloody two-by-four just in front of our feet. "Because you would have to have truly lost your mind to think you could get away with doing this."

What are you gonna do to me, is what I wanna ask. But it comes out as "So, what's gonna happen to me?"

She folds her hands in her lap.

"You gonna tell me to drop it too? Just like Moussa and Oumar and whoever the hell else is on my back about this? You gonna tell me not to look too deep into what happened to that girl because I might not like what I find? Because, Zoe, you and I both know what it was like before this city went up. What happened back then. Is what I'm doing really gonna screw up peace for all these people? Because shit doesn't look too peaceful right now. What should really be happ—"

She raises a hand and it slices off whatever the end of that sentence was gonna be.

"I'm sorry." And this time, I know what I'm apologizing for.

"You do know that I'm going to have to offer discounted prices tonight because of what you've done."

Which fills me with more shame than it should.

"I never thought you of all people would be the one to scare away my customers. Still." She gets up and dusts off stuff that isn't there. "You're coming with me."

"Why should I?"

Footsteps on the stairs. When the face they belong to appears, I try to figure out why it looks so familiar. Where have I seen that face before? Then I see the bracelets. One of the drummers from the campaign rally. Behind him, another figure. I've never seen her face before but when she turns to beckon more of her compatriots up the stairs, I catch the back of her head. I can't keep myself from gasping. The rally.

More and more people from the campaign rally ascend the stairs. I recognize only a few of them as drummers. The rest of them, I realize, were in the crowd. Then it hits me.

I didn't lose that doctor I was chasing because the crowd was too thick. I lost him because these people didn't want me to catch him. And now they're arrayed in front of me.

There's movement behind one of them, and he reaches behind him and swings a small form out in front of him.

It's the urchin he's got by the collar of his shirt. The kid's legs swing above the ground as he fights the big man's grip.

Zoe nods her head their way. "That's why."

CHAPTER TWENTY-THREE

We leave by the front. In full view of everyone downstairs and out on the street by the shisha spot. I'm behind Zoe. She leads the group. The folks from the rally look like somebody's honor guard. I can't tell if they belong to the candidate or they belong to Zoe. Bringing up the rear is the big guy who's still got the urchin by the collar.

Zoe doesn't seem to care that folks on the street are watching our procession. Hushed whispers follow us all the way down the strip. I know she's always been about her business, a no-nonsense type of dame. But there's a different seriousness about her now. A "no more screwing around" kind of energy.

I keep wanting to slow down so I can look natural, as I fall in step with the urchin. We have a lot to talk about, namely me trying to get him to calm down. Me trying to assure him that he's got nothing to worry about, Zoe won't let anything too terrible happen to him. But whenever I try to get close, the urchin's handler shoves me in the back, and I stumble forward. We do this little dance about three times before I give up. Maybe once we get to where we're headed, I can snatch a moment alone with the kid and we can compare notes on how we got here.

We round a corner that seems to come out of nowhere, just a corner like any other in the souq. But then we're passed into darkness. We keep marching, even over the urchin's protests. Then a lamp comes out of somewhere. Someone somewhere knocks three times on a metal door. A beat, something sliding.

Then the metal door grinds against the dirt, and we're moving again.

The hall we crowd into is just as dark, but eventually patches of colored light spread over the walls, then we hang a right into a nondescript room, a plain square box, with chipped concrete walls and a woman wearing a nomad's turban unraveled, cloth coming down both sides of her face and over her shoulders.

I get pushed forward, then the rest of the troop leaves.

"Hey!" I spin around. "Leave the kid al—" But one of the big rally drummers blocks the way. I try to shove the lady out the way, but somehow I'm on my ass and my cheek and left rib are on fire. I think my ankle's twisted too. I'm about to get up for round two when the lady behind me, the one with the unraveled turban, says, "You want to know about the girl?"

I whirl back around. "What did you say?"

She indicates the rug opposite her. There's a pot of tea on a raised tray and a small dish of chin-chin beside it. "Please." She says it like a command.

I sit. But I don't touch the tea. And hungry as I am, I don't touch the chin-chin either.

"Before you became a chercher, were you ever a cop?"

I try to place her voice, match it against anything in my memory. But I got nothing. This is a completely new person in my life. And I got no idea how to read her. "No."

"But you knew cops."

"Yeah."

"And you still know cops."

"One or two."

"Were they in the sorodassi with you?"

I make to get up, even though I have no intention of leaving this room. "This is pretty big for a kaso cell. But I ain't sign up for an interrogation."

"There is no other way for you to find what you're looking for than to sit here and talk with me."

"How do you know what I'm looking for?" I'm trying to draw her out, speed her past all the roadblocks and rabbit trails she's trying to put in my way, get straight to the heart of the matter. But I can tell, young as she looks, that she's not having it.

"Not once since being brought here have you asked me who I am."

I settle back in my seat. "Okay. Who are you?"

"My name is Kadiatou."

"Okay, Kadiatou. How do you know Zoe?"

"I'm a patron of her establishment, just like you."

"Havin' a hard time believing that's it."

"It's easy to think that being in a business means avoiding political matters. You think to yourself, no matter who my master is, everyone's going to need tea. Everyone's going to need shisha. Everyone's going to need mangoes. That doesn't stop because of this law or that law. You begin to think that commerce exists outside of the law, that it is bigger than the government. That you can live in the land of the merchants and not bother with the systems that govern the lives of the people you sell to. But the truly smart businesspeople, the truly smart store owners and merchants, they know that for the lie that it is. They know that it does matter who's in charge. Zoe is one such businessperson. For a long time, she has supported our efforts. Her donations to our political party and our leader's campaign have been invaluable. She is playing a great role in building the world that's to come."

"So she sends money your guy's way. Like a bribe." I raise an eyebrow. "In my experience, the bribe works best when the guy you're giving it to actually has power."

Now it's her turn to raise an eyebrow. "You don't think the Murutilen has power?"

"That's what you call him too?"

"Because of the Murutilen, half of the French Quarter hangs suspended from the sky."

I musta sat there with my jaw on the floor for a good ten minutes. That's certainly what it felt like. When I finally said, "What," my mouth was a desert.

"He did not command it. He did not bless it. But it was done in his name." She looks away.

"So . . . the jatigewalekela work for you?"

"It isn't the jatigewalekela who are responsible."

My jaw hurts.

"There is a militant wing to our party. That is, in fact, how we began. As a fighting force during the wars. But with stability, we needed new ways of combating the oppression enacted by the French. There was debate within the ranks. Then many of us broke away to form our political party. Where we would influence the workings of government through laws. Give our people a say in the way their lives are run. You cannot blow people up forever." She holds my gaze. "But there are some who still believe that is the way. Tea?"

I nod before I can stop myself. She pours a glass for each of us.

"They will say that they engage in their activities to throw off the yoke of oppression. To return us to our pastoral ways, bring back the dugu as it existed in the time before the French. But really they just want to take out their anger on something. And, well, explosions are cathartic." She takes a sip from her tea. "She was one such."

I don't have to ask who "she" is.

"There is no cure for the anger she felt. Her mind was never going to be changed. She would grow old hating the French."

I think of the old woman who shared her tea with me the day

of the attack on the French Quarter. "She never got to grow old, though." I sip my tea.

"No. She didn't."

"So she was a militant, then? Different from the jatigewalekela, you say." When Kadiatou nods, I continue. "And she hated the French. Though she wasn't responsible for the bombing of the French Quarter, because by then, she was dead." Kadiatou nods again. "So when she came to my place, the police were already on her trail."

"We presume so, yes."

"You don't think you all need to worry about that? About the police hounding you? Disrupting your . . . operations?"

"We are not our militant siblings."

"Bet you're not their keepers either."

Kadiatou bristles at the implication. "We serve all dugulenw."

"Yet you couldn't keep her from getting killed."

The look on Kadiatou's face isn't what I expected.

"You saying she wasn't killed?" I'm on my feet and almost knock over the tray. "She was hanging in the city square. Blood all around her. We all saw it."

"She wasn't murdered."

"What are you talking about?"

"Please retake your seat."

Stunned, I got no choice but to do what she says.

"She had a wound right along here, no?" And she draws a line along her abdomen. Horizontal. Right where the girl's wound was.

"Yeah, so?"

"She was a Floater." She waits for the shock to settle in. "She had an organ removed. It is unfortunately common among the more militant members of our ranks. They draw an incision and remove the organ responsible for processing water. It's . . . imagine a filtration device. The belief is that since the French arrived, they have poisoned our land and our water with their very presence. And slowly, we lost our ability to fly. Removing the organ is a way back. Removing the organ also turns the organ into a munition. They say they are donating their bodies to the revolution. And they are feted in the community as martyrs. The operation is . . . rarely successful." Something on my face stops her. "Are you all right?"

Too much is happening inside me. My head is a mess and my heart hurts.

"You know about Floating."

"She did it to herself?" I ask, more to shine the light away from me than anything else.

Kadiatou settles back in her seat. "Yes."

"And there was no way to fix it?" It'll kill me if it turns out there's something I coulda done for the girl. If she didn't absolutely have to end up the way she did.

"No. It is irreversible."

I can't help the chuckle that squirts out of me. I sniff. Wipe tears from my eyes. "All she wanted from me was to hide her." I shrug. "I tried. I tried to help her. That's all she wanted."

"No."

"What?"

"You're wrong."

"What? Wrong about what?"

"That's not what she wanted. She did not find you by accident."

"Find me? She knew who I was?"

"Yes. She knew who you were. The reason she came to you was so that she could kill you."

CHAPTER TWENTY-FOUR

"The reason she came to you was so that she could kill you."

So that's it, then. It wasn't chance. It wasn't bad luck. It was a plan. The girl knew her time was up. Had one last thing to take care of. And it was right there, standing over her, looking her in the eye, helping her hide. But then she caught some of my bad luck. Soon as she came into my orbit, it all must've fallen apart for her. Almost closed the circle. If she'd done it, she probably coulda died happy. Or as close to happy as her type can get. "Why?" The question's out of my mouth before I can figure out why I asked it.

There's a lot to read in Kadiatou's face. But I catch a trace of pity. She doesn't know why I asked either. "Come with me," she says.

More dark corridors, more hushed conversation I don't even catch pieces of. But some doors we pass are cracked open just a bit. And I can note that light glows from a lamp in a small circle to illuminate figures talking urgently over a table. Some people eye me warily, but most don't. That's how you know these aren't the militants. They're not trying to hide anything from me.

We get outside and that dusk wind is a cold slap to the face. It's even got my dirty djellaba whipping about me. But we get to a ladder and climb until we're roofside. The city and the expanse beyond it sprawl before us.

For a while, Kadiatou stands alone at the roof's edge, hands clasped behind her. I join her and that's when I notice that a number of her confederates have come up the ladder behind us. They keep their distance, though. A couple of 'em are the same that "escorted" me and the urchin here. Maybe they're Kadiatou's honor guard. Or maybe this party just shares them, loans them out to whoever needs to look intimidating to their prisoner. Neat reminder that I never stopped being their prisoner.

The sunset's far enough along that it makes the horizon look like it's bleeding while the city and the Ethnic Quarter are the color of a bruise.

"Do you see it?" Kadiatou asks.

"See what?"

She waits a minute. Then she points. And there it is. Adam Island. From here, you can see a little bit more of the construction surrounding the housing development. Far away like this, I still feel the same coal-quick rage I felt last time I saw those apartments. But distance muffles the fire a little. A little.

"Yeah, I see it."

"I don't think you do." She points to another spot far to the right. It's another batch of houses and apartments. Had no idea it was out there. Then she points to another, and it's like half a ring around the Ethnic Quarter. Distant with enough space in between to draw lines for several football pitches. But stand on a high enough hill and you'd see the cranes and all that machinery just fine. "And there." She points to another.

"Ain't enough français to live in them right now. They all got funny names?"

She shoots me a frown. But she doesn't know where my impulse to make jokes comes from. Maybe she does and doesn't care. "They call that one Adam Island. But its true name is Bamako. That one to the right of it is Ouagadougou. Sikasso. Gao. Diapaga."

"They're getting closer."

"That's not the important part."

"What are you talking about?"

"Those aren't housing developments. Those are crime scenes." She turns to face me. Part of her gown detaches to reveal a cape that whips in the wind around her. Entirely too dramatic. "This is how the diéman erase evidence of their crimes."

"I don't—"

"Under each of those housing developments is a village of bones. Those homes, they sit on mass graves." She looks over her shoulder at me. "During the war, operations were launched to clear those villages. Apparently, the French sorodassi believed there were militants in those villages. What they called terrorists. And so they shot and bayonetted and burned down everything they could find. Whatever would fit in their sacks or on their carts, they stole." She turns back to the hidden atrocities. "Our party's mission is exposing the truth. It is important we keep these memories alive."

"For the Commission."

"Yes."

"The Commission that only happens if your man wins."

"Yes." She bows her head, sighs, then looks back up. "Yes. The Commission that only happens if the Murutilen wins." It's more than confidence that I hear in her voice. Sounds like something I've heard plenty in my days, something I've heard plenty of over the past forty-eight hours. Sounds like a threat. She must be able to read my posture, 'cause she then says, "You needn't worry, Boubacar. We are very invested in keeping you alive. Our aim to reveal the truth of what happened during the war is greatly weakened absent your testimony."

Someone I don't recognize comes up behind Kadiatou and whispers in her ear, glances at me, then retreats into the shadows.

Without looking at me, she says, "There was an attempt made on your friend's life."

"Moussa?"

"Your friend in the convalescent home."

Oumar.

"He is fine. He, just like you, has a role to play in serving our purpose."

I grit my teeth. "He know you got these plans for him?"

"He does."

"What happens?" I ask her.

"When what?"

"What happens when whatever truth you think you're gonna find there comes out? Say there was some state-sanctioned whatever, and it comes out that the French wiped out entire villages. What happens then? What changes?" I can tell I'm getting angry, angry past any point I'm trying to make, angry for angry's sake. "You think all them young français kissing and making babies and getting rich in those new apartments are going to slap their foreheads in shock that that's what made their lives possible? You think the government's gonna say 'sorry' or that the king's even gonna apologize for his part? What changes? How does this make any dugulen's life better?"

She says nothing. Not because I've caught her off guard. But because she's seen this too many times before. She's just waiting for me to tire myself out. Like a kid having a tantrum.

"You know, before all of this, I thought she was being hunted by a killer. That's what I thought this was. I thought it was some diéman going through the Ethnic Quarter carving up boys and girls and somehow getting them to hang in the air like that. And, to be honest, that was—"

"Easy."

That brings me up short. "Yeah. Easy."

Her voice lowers but somehow becomes that much clearer. "Sometimes the virtue in knowing a thing isn't to make money from it or to improve your material circumstances. Sometimes it is enough to know a thing."

"The girl knew and look where it got her."

"We are not all her."

"How do you know?"

She smirks at me, but there's a shit-ton of sadness in it. Pity too, I think.

"You think whoever went after Oumar is gonna come after me too?"

"Going to?"

I let out a bitter chuckle. Of course people been after me already. If it's not for one thing, it's for another. Loans, historical reckoning. Same thing, right?

"So now you know what it's all about. You know why she died. You know what she was after. What will you do?"

It's a good question. Doesn't happen often, but sometimes a case gets solved for me. Either the people paying me find the answer on purpose because they're so annoying and enterprising, or they find it by accident. A cupboard they hadn't searched before holding a ring, or a note someone had errantly kicked under the stairs. Or maybe someone in the family or at the workplace finally speaks up, long after I've gotten involved. More often than not, I still got paid. So I didn't mind not being the one to deliver the news. The job wasn't like that. Wasn't my everything. Was just a way to keep debt collectors off my back. And I happened to be halfway decent at it. But this one's different. Not just because I've been getting my shit kicked for free. It's the closest I ever been to what I was looking for. Odd way of putting it, but that's what it feels like. Her not getting closure somehow means I don't get closure either. You could give me all the words in both my languages, and I couldn't explain it to you. Just what it is.

"Hm," Kadiatou says when I keep quiet.

She clears her throat, then puts on gloves and lashes her cape closer to her. We're finished here.

I wasn't entirely truthful to Kadiatou up on that rooftop. At the time, I didn't know what I was gonna do. By the time I'm out onto the street, though, I know exactly who I need to see next.

CHAPTER TWENTY-FIVE

"You'd be a much prettier man if you gave half a damn."

I should feel ashamed sitting across from Aissata like this. Me with my dirt-and-blood-stained djellaba and a floppy, crooked cap I found in a pocket. Her in a slim-fitting white robe with floral patterns framed by crossed swords coming down the front. Her wrists ring with bangles. Though her hair is in hijab, that doesn't keep me—or anyone—from being able to see the emeralds hanging from her ears. "When's the last time you saw a chercher who was good at his job and pretty?"

"And yet here you are, smelly and without a case in sight." It'd be mean coming from anyone else, but it gets me chuckling. I don't even mind she made us both sit in these high-backed chairs with a whole wooden desk between us.

It's fully night outside, but you can't tell from the way the hanging lamps along the spread-out walls light the room up. Aissata called this a levée, which doesn't make sense because it's about time for most people to be going to sleep.

"It's this new thing the king's doing. Gets up in the morning, invites his friends in to watch him dress. And as he puts on his socks or his garters or whatever the hell it is he's wearing these days, he listens to complaints." Aissata had her cheek against her fist, but this gets her barking out a laugh. "Imagine that." Though she's getting up in years, Aissata's still a twist and a half. Strong jawline and an angular face that leaves plenty of space for dimples deep enough to lose a finger in. Even in a military uniform, coordinating supply chains for the rest of us, she cut a pretty stunning figure. Younger, when her form was a little less severe, "Ishtar" is what visitors from the East would call her. Then they'd spend a good fifteen minutes trying to pick their jaws up off the floor. Made the femme fatale thing easier. I was never a mark, because there was no way I could make her rich. But between then and here, quite a few rich men ended up in a garden. "Imagine beginning your day with violence."

"Couldn't be me," I chuckle. She's got kafe out, which means this ain't a formal thing, and she's got no pretensions of what kind of host she needs to be here. This is old friends chopping grass together. After the meal when you pick your teeth with your nail and loosen your belt and sprawl on your couch or floor or chaise longue and catch up. "Couldn't be me."

"So I hear you've been stirring things up," she says around the français hanging with heartbreaking elegance from her lips.

I grab a candle dish on her desk and bring it to her face. She coulda just as easily bent forward and lit the français herself, but I felt moved. And there's something about this woman that brings out the people-pleaser in me. She looks me in the eye when that happens and I'm sent all the way back to the first time I saw her, almost two decades ago, nervously getting her instructions in a row of gowned girls while I with my newly issued cutlass and uniform marched by. We both did our double take. And that's when we knew we had to make that moment again as many times as we could. Closest I ever came to falling in love, and it all comes flooding back into my chest in that moment my dumb ass decides to be a gentleman and light this woman's cigarette.

She leans back first and that's my cue to get back into my seat. I'm still perched forward, forearms on my thighs, though. Because I can't ever tell this dame I'm not interested in her. She's got the français in a small holder, taps the ash from time to time

in a bronze ashtray. "I should've known when strange things began happening here that you were involved."

"Aissata. That ain't fair." I try to sound like I'm joking. And
really it ain't fair, because it isn't just me swallowed up in this
thing. Ask me to define "thing" here and you'd get pretty much a
shrug from me. But so far, it's been all of us who straddle the line
between both worlds who I've been coming across here. Moussa
is a policier, Zoe's apparently a political donor, Zanga is maybe
a heavy and a smuggler for a French developer, and Aissata's the
dugulen who made it big after the war. During it too, if we're
being honest. If you were gonna be mean about it, you'd call it
war profiteering, but we all know she was just doing what it took
to get out of where she was. Where we were. And that brings
us here. Brings me here. Chasing a lead to a case that's already
closed. A mystery that's already solved. But I can't stop. Not now.
Still feels incomplete.

"You have that look again," she tells me.

"What look?"

"You're imagining the bone you're going to be chewin' the
hell off of in about fifteen minutes."

"Nobody knows me as well as you."

She smirks. "I know."

I'm itching for a français, just to match her energy, but I got
none on me and I don't wanna put her out more than she already
is. If Kadiatou's right about people being after me, I'm putting
Aissata in danger right now. Then again, Aissata used to smuggle
weapons and gold, so who's to say Aissata would even notice? I
manage to tamp down the desire for a smoke just barely. "You're
plugged into all this business stuff way more than I am. Say I
wanted to buy a plot of land, build on it. You know, with all the
French laws and all that."

"Are we getting out of the game?"

"I'm getting old, Aissata. Stopped being a game a while back. I just wanna retire, you know. Leave the city behind for a bit. Leave it all behind. It's not going anywhere. Any time I need that smoke in my eyes, I know where to go. But say a guy wanted to build a home for himself out past the city limits, maybe something big enough to hold a family, how would he go about it?"

She's smiling at me, but there's something stern or wary or hurt behind it. I can't tell. "Who's the lucky girl?"

"Eh, you don't know her."

"I probably do." There it is again.

"No, it's no one. She's . . . there's no she. I just . . . I dunno, maybe one day I'll get lucky." And this time I hold her gaze. "Maybe I'll be able to charm a princess out of her castle. Put her roots back in the soil. I'd have to be pretty good, though. Because I don't know that this house would be able to fit all her diamonds and all her paintings. All that fancy wooden furniture and all that. I'd have to be really. Really. Good. And lucky." I settle back in my chair and turn it back off. She just needs to know I still got it. And that there's space in my heart, maybe my future too, for her. Been keeping it warm all this time, just never had the stones to tell her. Maybe when this is all over . . . Let me stop myself there.

There's a moment where she squints. And I can tell she's trying to figure me out, untangle all that stuff that just happened. But she also knows me well enough to know that when I close a window or seal a well, it stays that way till I decide otherwise. "You'd look at the property records to see who already owns that land. Those are in the Mize, top floor. But you know all that already."

"What I don't know about yet is Adam Island. Who's Honoré Mirbeau de L'Isle-Adam?"

Aissata sniffs, looks away. If it were a different time, she probably woulda spit in her ashtray.

"Guy's got developments all over the place outside the city. He pick those places on purpose or by accident?"

"What are you implying?"

"I'm trying to figure out what he's after. He just wanna make more money? Is that it? Why would he put those developments so far outside the city? What's he after?"

Aissata shrugs. I wonder if it hurts her somewhere tiny and quiet that I'm asking her of all people this. Like because she has money she's animated by the same stuff that gets Honoré up every morning, taking meetings in his levée. "Maybe it's a distraction."

"What do you mean?"

"He's got a private security force he leases to the Kingsguard. They patrol the Ethnic Quarter, and the French government doesn't have to get its hands dirty with enforcement. All that money goes to Honoré. And they go around ripping hijab off the girls, keeping the dugulenw from the ballot box. How do you think Ibrahim Savadogo won that first election? Everyone knew who he was the second he announced his candidacy. And there were certainly enough voting-age dugulenw to keep him from becoming president. Still are. But Honoré . . . men like him, they get their money and their desire changes form. You have all the chicken you could ever eat, all the légumes, so you want the weather. That's what it is with him. It's all about the power. He wants to know that he is the wind. Knocking people down or holding them up. And he thinks fiddling with an election is the way to do it. Thinks fiddling with this one'll do it too."

"You think he'll win? Savadogo? Or is your money on the Murutilen?"

Aissata's eyebrows rise. A surprised chuckle slips from her lips. "You call him that too?"

I shrug. "It's contagious. Spend any time in the souq, and it just may happen to you too." I'm hunched over the edge of her desk, thinking and looking kind of childish about it. "So. This Honoré Mirbeau de L'Isle-Adam, he someone I can ask about property?"

"What, like an audience?"

"Yes, like an audience."

"There's no levée with him. Most of high society has no idea what he looks like."

"But."

"But there's a donor dinner tomorrow night. Honoré is bringing together all the major aristocrats and societymen who've contributed to Savadogo's campaign so far. As well as some of the propagandists who fancy themselves independent artists and poets."

"You sayin' that's my ticket? That sounds like it'd be harder to get into, if I'm being honest."

"Oh, they'll be excited to see you. If your goal is to get a minute or two with Honoré, getting to him won't be your problem. Picking your way through all the folks curious about you might."

"Why would folks be curious about—"

But she's already standing by now. She stubs out her français and runs her hands along her gown, smoothing it, accentuating the curves. "When Paul died, I kept his clothes. We'll have you washed and fitted in the morning." She extends a hand.

"You know," I say to her hand. To her eyes, I say, "Nobody's ever showed me a kindness like you did. Whole time we've known each other, it's been you."

"I know. Now come to bed."

CHAPTER TWENTY-SIX

There are too many strangenesses to count in Honoré Mirbeau de L'Isle-Adam's sprawling dining room. First off, it beggars belief that this is all just one room. You could fit a whole Murutilen rally in here. Have all their voices bouncing in echo off the vaulted ceilings. Second, a fire burns in a fireplace tended to, almost invisibly, by dugulenw dressed in finery. Chandeliers hang over the long rectangular table we're all supposed to sit at at some point in the evening. Giant paintings, practically life-size, line the walls. Serveurs carry trays of animal parts wrapped up in leaves soaked in animal juice. Or something like that. But the strangest thing of all is that Honoré Mirbeau de L'Isle-Adam is brown.

"Are you sure that's our guy?" I ask Aissata out of the side of my mouth while she looks hungrily at the room over the lip of her champagne flute. "That's the Adam Island guy?"

"You see why he's so good at hiding? Could be standing right there in plain sight and no one would assume that this tiny brown man owns a quarter of the kingdom. In fact—"

"So *this* is the new beau, Aissata?" It's a nasal voice coming from behind. There's a papery-feeling hand on my shoulder. I stuff down the instinct to put the body it belongs to on its ass. Instead, I turn and I'm staring a grinning, skinny, bejeweled diéman in the face, his brown curls framing his face like a screwed-up lion's mane. "Cleans up nicely, but still a bit rough around the edges, non?"

Aissata smiles deeply into the man's face, leans toward him

too. "Rough is more your bailiwick, Gustave." Then to me, "Babe, this is Gustave. He'll insist he's a marquis from the home country, but really it's half an estate. At least until he murders his cousin."

"Aissa!" Gustave gasps, looking very aghast at Aissata. "All my business for this newcomer to gawk over."

That's not what I'm gawking over.

"Well, Monsieur, consider yourself fully indoctrinated. Is that the word? Inculcated? Indicated? Well, I'm sure you know what I mean. Aisse, he looks like one of the smart ones. Don't break him, I might want to see him again." Then the drunk français with the curly lion's mane is off, talking about me too loudly to a crowd of françaises in bouffants.

I realize I don't have my glass anymore, must've misplaced it. It wasn't for drinking anyway, just to figure out what to do with my hands as this very pretty thing I'm wearing has no pockets to be seen. But to my rescue comes a liveried servant with a train of flutes. I grab one, breathless with gratitude, and our eyes meet and I wonder what he's trying to ask me or tell me in that brief instant before he's gone. Be careful? I know you're an impostor? I'm jealous of you and want to murder you and wear your skin? Could be any or all of the above. But that's not my problem at the moment.

"Looks like a path has been cleared," Aissata whispers to me. I follow her gaze. The circle of bonhommes around Honoré has dispersed. Time to go in for the kill. "I've some conversation to make."

"Thank you," I tell her.

"Why, for what?"

"Serving yourself up like this. As a distraction."

"Oh, honey. Is that what you think I'm doing? I'm working, babe. There are shipping contracts to secure. Do you think I'd just let all these housing developments get filled with young French families with no food to eat? Someone has to get paid for feeding those kids." She's smiling and speaking in that deep voice of hers when she murmurs all of this to me. And I can tell she's given me all these details to disabuse me of any notions of altruism. She's just as deep in the shit as the rest of us. The last thing she wants for me is to think she's got clean hands in this. But perhaps to lick some sting off of it all, she brings me in for a kiss and tongues her way past my teeth. It's not love, it's showing off. It's telling the gathered folk who have the indecency to look that I'm the best lay in the land. Then she breaks away. "Go get 'im, tiger."

Takes less than a second to straighten myself, clear my throat, all of that. But I'm barely two steps out before some other mook crashes right into me. I'm trying to shake my right sleeve dry when I look up and see it's the serveur from before. "What're you doin', man? Come on."

When the other folks look our way, I realize it isn't because of the commotion. It's because I'm not mean enough to the guy. Even if he did this on purpose—and I'm halfway sure he did— I'm not tryna get this dugulen fired. He's probably all sorts of confused, straddling these two worlds. Maybe he even lives somewhere in this building or out back, completely separate from whoever once upon a time knew him in the Ethnic Quarter. Thinks he's one thing when really he's two others.

But some diéman saves the day. My life and probably the serveur's. Comes in between me and my nemesis, pulls a gilt-edged kerchief from his breast pouch and attentively dabs at my nipple. "Here, Monsieur. Right this way. If we're going to get you cleaned up, we shouldn't also be blocking traffic in the bargain."

"Much obliged," I say to the long-haired guy fussing over the wine on my shirt. "Hey, you're good. You can stop now."

The guy looks up at me, almost like he's seeing my face for the first time, then he stuffs the stained kerchief in a pocket out of sight. "But of course." Then he settles in next to me. Doesn't give his name or anything, but acts like we're already close enough that we can look at the gathered folks with an air of conspiracy about us. "It is odd and yet oddly reaffirming."

"What is?" Part of me tries to affect a higher-pitched, softer voice like I've never done an honest day's work in my life, but then halfway through, I give up. Let this exotic and rakish charm that all these folks believe I have be the thing to get me through this.

"That they're all people at the end of the day. No smarter, no more blessed by divine providence, no stronger. Just people who happened to have guns and a purely mercantile viewpoint on how the world should operate." He rests an arm on my shoulder. Though there's wine on his breath, he sounds sober as an avalanche. "I know what you are."

I gesture at the milling mass of français chatting and arguing and laughing through their jowls and their wigs and their collars. "I bet you your estate all of them out there know too."

"Oh, I don't have an estate. I'm a mere poet and philosopher. Why angle for an estate when you can have a patron instead? Moonlighting as a muse is to bask in the perpetual sunlight of a wealthy man's attentions. Lucrative sunlight too." The kid is young, though he's as tall as me. Maybe a little taller. And I'm sure other français would fancy him pretty. He seems like the type they would go for if they weren't trying to climb dugulenw towers.

"Gun's a pretty big difference between us and them."

"Well, it most certainly isn't the only one."

"Shit, you might be on to something."

The poet-slash-philosopher doesn't seem to appreciate my tone. "What I mean is that, even without the gun, I think they would be the same. What your people call the diéman. The whites." He draws even closer to me, gestures to the crowd of men, Aissata among them making it all look so easy. "I'm sure you're cognizant of what it took for them to get here, to get all of this. How much blood it cost to buy."

I mime a sip to give myself something to do. "Yeah. It's crossed my mind."

"Do you think you'd be capable of the same?"

I go to mime another sip, but I stop. It's a better question than it sounds.

"Do you? Could you imagine you or your people doing to the diéman, doing to anyone in the world, really, what we've done to you? My whole profession is about plumbing the depths of human psychology, swimming through human experience and history to figure out the why and the how of it all, and this is what I find myself circling: our uniquely pathological capacity for violence."

"I think you might be missing a few steps in there," I tell him, but I do think he's on to something. I seen dugulenw hurt each other, do truly heinous, evil things. But could the dugulenw en masse ever look at the diéman the way they look at us? Could we ever look past them the way they look past us? Why was it so easy for me to imagine a diéman running through the Ethnic Quarter carving up dugu women? Why was it so difficult to imagine them doing that to themselves?

"I'd hoped you might be able to provide some insight. An outside perspective. We so rarely get your kind in our midst. At least, those exemplars of your people not confined to the serving professions. Not afraid to speak your mind. Someone who doesn't see the threat of a guillotine around every corner." He laughs, airily and loud at the same time. Then he looks me up and down. "It was a pleasure. An absolute pleasure." Doesn't even ask my name before he leaves.

At the far end of the room, a figure makes to disappear around a corner.

I make a dash for it. If I'm fast enough, I can catch him and cause as little disturbance as possible. But when I get to the end of another hallway, two giant Kingsguardsmen block my path to the double doors Honoré's in the middle of passing through. Before any of the four of us can think, I twist the fingers of one, take his spear and trip the other, smacking both on the back of the head so that they fall limp.

Honoré, caught in the doorway, half of him in the safety of his room, half of him hanging out in the hallway, looks at me with undisguised horror.

"I got some questions for you, brown man," I tell him, more winded than I care to admit. "Why don't you prepare us some tea?"

CHAPTER TWENTY-SEVEN

I'm still kinda winded from giving those guards the business, but I manage to keep my spear arm steady.

"Take a seat, Honoré Mirbeau de L'Isle-Adam."

He's a chubby mouse of a guy, soft fingers and palms, a little bit of baby fat still in his cheeks. Salt-and-pepper stubble. But it's a plain robe over his bony shoulders, tan with vertical red stripes meeting at the center just above his belly button. And he's only got maybe a few rings on the fingers of his left hand. No more jewelry than that. But it reminds me of something Aissata told me when we lay in her four-poster bed together, tangled up in sheets I woulda had to work a year's worth of cases straight to afford: wealthy men announce their status, powerful men don't.

"Go on." I hold the spear out and gesture to one of those high-backed chairs in front of his desk. It's facing the desk, so when he sits down he has to put his back to me. But I circle around, spear pointed at him the whole time, and I take my own seat behind the desk. I make a whole show of putting the spear down right within my reach, spearpoint aimed straight at the guy's heart. This way, I got a clear look at both him and the door. For when those guards wake up.

There was a moment by the door when I saw genuine fear in those eyes. His breath quickened and everything, shoulders hitched up, all of that. But now, he's the picture of calm. Has his hands folded in his lap, breath coming and going like there's a summer breeze kissing his cheeks right now.

"Don't tell me you know everything about me too."

"Excuse me?"

"You haven't somehow been tracking me? Trying to get rid of me or to manipulate me into doing one thing or another?"

"Sir, I have no idea whatsoever what to which you refer."

I blink my surprise at him. "Past week, everybody's got some way of surprising me, lettin' me know they've tracked my every move or they know what I've been looking for or they've seen me do this or heard I was askin' about that. I just figured . . . maybe you mighta heard about me."

His eyebrows rise, but other than that, not an inch of him moves. "I've never seen you before in my life."

"Okay, well, then I know quite a bit about you." I lean forward on the desk. I still got a quick line on the spear if I need it. "Like all your housing developments circling the Ethnic Quarter. Those are yours, right? Don't bother lying, because I've seen the property records."

"The developments do have my name on them."

"So that's all you, then. You're financing all those housing developments. All those lily-white français know their coin's going into the pocket of a dugulen?"

For a long time, he's quiet. He doesn't smirk, doesn't smile. Doesn't do any traditional villain things. Doesn't even look at me like I'm a five-year-old putting his baby toes in the water for the first time. "They don't need to know who I am. And even if they did, this younger generation, what is this place to them? A frontier? A chance to repair a marriage? An opportunity to make your own fortune? Maybe they'll start a mine. Maybe they'll get into import-export. Maybe they'll find a way to bottle up the exoticisms of this place and ship them back to the metropole at a hefty profit for all their friends and family who couldn't afford to make the journey. If they think dugu sand will get their trees to flourish or dugu herbs will cure their tuberculosis, who am I to get in their way? Leave them to their superstitions. And, besides, these new français, they're not like dugu children, always being taught by their parents or grandparents who wronged whom, which cousin is feuding with which cousin. The diéman want only to feel good. So why should it matter who is the instrument for the actualization of that fact?"

It can't be all as simple as that. And yet, what's a big enough and simple enough justification for all of this? What's a big enough force to move all of our worlds like this, crash us all together like this, crush us underfoot? Diéman wanna feel good so dugulenw get bottled up in the Ethnic Quarter. Diéman wanna feel good so dugulenw gotta carve themselves up because the water's poisoned. Diéman wanna feel good so a girl who wants to kill me can't get her closure before she closes her eyes forever. "Somethin' about this isn't making sense."

He hasn't moved, but he looks now like a guy at ease. Like he ain't being held hostage by a stranger right now. "Yes?"

"That warehouse to the north and west of the French Quarter. That ain't have your name on it."

Is he tensing? The end of his sleeves, dark with sweat?

"But it's yours all the same. Property records tell me as much."

Nothing.

"How come that's the bit of info that's got you all clammed up now? You ain't got no disquisitions on human nature to spill out anymore? Nothin' about what diéman want and how that's what makes the world go 'round?" I lean back but all the while I got half an eye on the spear. "After all this, you're still worried about incriminating yourself. But it's just me and you in here."

"Whatever you're implying, do be clearer about it."

"I think you knew what that warehouse was being used for."

This is the first time I'm saying it out loud and it has that scary feel of permanence to it. Like, I can't take it back afterward. Whether I'm wrong or I'm right, once this accusation's out there, it stops being speculation in my head. Starts being something harder and more dangerous.

Just in case, I wait to see if he'll jump out in front of it. Say something to implicate himself and inadvertently spare me the burden of laying the stake in the sand. But he's silent.

"Jatigewalekela or some other group, you knew they were using your warehouse to launch a terrorist operation." No tell, no twitch, no nothing. He's too good at it, trying too hard. That's how I know he's guilty as hell. "How much of it can you see from here?" I nod at the window behind me without taking my eyes off him. "Is it still mostly in the air? Nobody in your little dining room will say, but the past few days, I've heard people saying things. Talking about how, randomly, they'll hear crashes. Giant crashes. Thunderclaps. And it's someone's front porch falling out of the sky. Half a house. You don't hear the softer ones. The body that's rotted beyond recognition in the heat. Those don't make a sound when they land. Whoever did that used your warehouse to do it. Now what I don't get is why you'd let that happen. If all you're about is making a buck off the français, why let them get blown up like this?"

"You're deux-fois." His lips curl into a sneer when he says it.

"Yeah, so?"

"All those rooms you can walk into . . . simply because you have their nose or their eyebrows or their chin. You put on an outfit like this, and suddenly, you are one of them. It is not the français who make their putrid jokes about you, it's the dugu-lenw. Every dugulen you see in these rooms is a collection of horrible decisions that had to be made, pieces of their life sliced off and left to putrefy in the sun, bargains made, pools bathed in. For access. Nothing more than access. But you. Tu fais le grand écart."

"So you hate them, then. Is that why you let that attack happen?"

His laugh is bitter. Feels like now that he's bared his soul to me, he feels no more impulse to hide his intentions. His plan, none of that. "Hate them? You've got it all wrong. The diéman are the future. You may look at me and think, 'pfft, some other self-styled entrepreneur who thinks that if he rubs himself with enough coins, he will turn white,' but I could care less about becoming them. They are the future, because the world they are making is the future. The dugu is a thing of the past. All these ways people try to cling to it, you are fighting a tidal wave."

"That why you have goons caning girls for wearing hijab? That why you're intimidating dugulenw into staying home from the election?"

He waves that away. Like harassing dugu girls into forcefully forgetting their culture is a mosquito in his ear.

"So you know what you're building on, yes?"

"Those claims are unproven. There is no evidence that those building sites are where wartime massacres happened. None whatsoever."

"Guess we'll never know, will we? Not like those young French families are getting displaced any time soon." Then I realize, "You never answered my question. Why'd you let the attack on the French Quarter happen? What'd you gain from that?"

For the first time during out whole chat, he lets himself look smug. "Surely you saw the aftermath."

"Yeah, dugulenw all up and down the city got their asses beat."

"And their presidential candidate, who has been trying to

spread his message of peace and reconciliation, cannot be heard over the sound of militant grumbling."

"If he wins, that Truth and Reconciliation project of his is gonna dig up those plots of land." I can't help but gasp. "You're not gonna take that chance, are you?" Suddenly, I'm up, over the desk, and with the spear tip pointed at his throat. "How's it gonna happen? How are you gonna do it?"

"I don't know." He's not saying it like he's pleading for his life. He's saying it like it wouldn't matter whether he knew or not; it would still get done. "But the call to the mogofagala has already been made. He won't know to expect it. No one protecting him will know. Nor will I. We will all simply wake up one morning to news that the Murutilen is no longer breathing."

I have to warn Kadiatou and the others.

But first I have to figure out what to do about the gendarmes who've just burst through the door. And the guns they have aimed straight at my head.

CHAPTER TWENTY-EIGHT

The first shot wings my cheek, but only because I slip out of the way in time. The second hits window glass. By then, I'm behind the desk.

I've lost sight of Honoré. Can't hear his voice above the shouted commands and the reports of gunfire. Couldn't get a good look at the door before they opened fire, so I've got no idea how many shooters are now filling the room. More could've come in by now. If I were a more traditional warrior type, I would've trained my ears to listen for footfalls, tracking each gendarme's different pattern of walking or stomping. Or I'd be able to distinguish the different tones and timbres of their French voices, but it's all a cloud of shouting and shooting and stomping to me. Smoke starts to fill the room. Soon as I go to peek out over the desk, another blast from someone's hand cannon and that whole chunk of desk evaporates. I get sent to the floor. Feeling stupid as hell for holding on to this spear the way that I am.

Another shot takes out another chunk of desk. The sounds of glass shattering, scrabbling of cloth and knees against tiled floor. A painting falls to the floor. Other than that, soundlessness. I make a dash for the window. And I don't know why, but I chance a look behind me. And see a hand cannon aimed right at the space between my eyes.

"Hey!" a voice shouts from the doorway.

The shot goes high. Glass rains on me. I hit the floor. There's a bloody hand right in my line of sight. A gendarme. When did that happen? I have my back up against the remains of a cupboard. Try to look over at the door. Nearly catch wood chips from the desk in my eye. But now the gunfire's going two different ways. There's someone on the other side of that portal helping a brother out. I wonder if she's gone to any pains to hide her face or disguise herself or if she doesn't care. Maybe she doesn't mind folks knowing it's me she's helping out. Then it hits me that if Honoré goes down, she's pretty much taken out her last major competition in the whole, well, import-export business. She knew exactly what she was doing bringing me here. Gotta hand it to her. Ruthless as they come, that one.

I still wanna head her way, if for no other reason than to be a dumbass and give her a dramatic kiss. But that would defeat the whole point of her distracting them for me. I hook my fingers in the sash of the dead gendarme by my desk and pull him over. Hand cannon and two charges. That'll have to do. I'll have to be fast, though.

I load a charge, hook the spear behind me, and whirl around to shoot blindly at some bit of floor at the center of the chaos. Not tryna kill anyone, just cause some more chaos. Then I head for the window fast as my legs'll take me and crash through what's left of the glass.

Blast of cold air hits my face and my body. Hits my chest too, knocks all the air out of my lungs. For a second, I'm mad at Aissata that she ain't let me put on something a little baggier, something that didn't hug my gut the way this thing is now. More fabric would've allowed for some wind resistance too, because now, I'm heading straight for this watermelon cart like a rock.

Little bit of updraft does nothing to keep this from being the hardest, wettest splat of my life. I'm surprised the cart itself didn't buckle under me. But, looking around at the massacre—the evidence of which I'm wearing on my shirt—well, there's nothing here I'd sell in good conscience to someone else.

I can't hear any of the ruckus from all the way down here. And it's only in looking back up that I realize how far I've fallen.

But then cannon fire explodes a melon right by my head. Seeds slice at the side of my face. I roll over onto the ground. On my hands and knees under the cart, I see—guess what? More gendarmes. I reach above my head for the hand cannon, surely somewhere in the cart among the mess of shattered melons, but then another shot nearly takes my hand off. And, of course, my spear is nowhere in sight.

Soon as I try to run, though, I realize I'm not made of stone. One leg gives out under me, and I gotta claw and scrape my way back onto one knee.

Being on this side of the city at night is never not strange. The noises and the partying, it's all kept behind windows. In individual rooms, and maybe you can see the lights from the streets. Hear the muffled giggles and the loud shouting of play-arguments. But none of it spills onto the streets. On the streets, you can hear every crime the police are about to stop. Just as I'm sure you can hear the footsteps of the gendarmes closing in on their subject. I stagger a few more steps before I see half a dozen in front of me, fanned out to encircle me. A mirror image of the group behind me. All with their hand cannons raised. Their swords all within reach for when the time comes. They probably don't even know what I did. But a man falling onto a cart of watermelons was probably never up to any good.

I slowly raise my arms in surrender. There's nowhere for me to go. Everywhere's blocked off. The whole cobblestoned street is open, empty of any and all potential distractions. No errant horse-drawn cart. No urchins to draft into your service. No roof-top angel to help engineer an escape. Nobody out on the street to see what they can do for a neighbor in distress. Sounds pretty much like the future Honoré's so intent on making real.

They all close in at once. This bunched up, there's no use in having their hand cannons out. Instead, one of them brings out rope and binds my wrists behind me. I wonder what French jail's gonna be like. A dungeon? Or more like one of those levées Aissata was talking about? With a bed and a place for your friends to sit while you hear their complaints? Maybe a stool to put your feet up on while your shoes get shined. Someone hits the back of my knee and I collapse like the bottom went out of a sack of rocks. That was my bad knee too.

Who am I kidding? At this point, they're both my bad knee.

They pull me upright. Right eye won't open all the way. One of them stands right in front of me. I hear something click and whoosh, look up to see him removing a face guard. There's no beard, just a small mustache that could belong to someone my son's age, if I had a son.

"Where are the rest of them?"

They're really gonna interrogate me in the middle of the street. "Don't know what you're talking ab—"

A gauntleted hand smacks loose a tooth. I cough for good measure, work it loose, then spit it out.

Then I sigh, ready for the next blow.

"Where are your confederates?"

"Don't know what you're talking a—"

And another one. When I'm straight again, he looks over my head at someone behind me.

"Hey, wh—" But the garrote's already over my throat. In-stantly, I try to push onto my feet, but whoever's got the ligature yanks me back so that I'm on my ass. My wrist bends bad. Pain shoots up my elbow. My fingers are at my throat, trying to get under the cord while my feet shoot out and my heels scrape themselves bloody against the stones. Everything comes out of my throat as a gurgle. It feels like they're slicing it open and pulling it apart with their fingers. Hands hold down my legs, even while I kick and squirm. I can't see who those hands belong to. Things are going dark at the corners.

Not sure why this is the one that really spooks me. I've been shot at before, cut. People've tried to strangle me. I've had my head in a river once or twice, not by choice. Sure, I might've been feeling whatever invincibility kick I was on at the time. Being too young to think you'll die, being so fed up with life you're always asking for it, being experienced enough at your job that you fancy you've seen just about every angle it can come from. I thought that was it. But I'm here with my hands bound, one wrist broken, my legs held down, and a murderous Frenchman digging a cord into my neck with all his strength. And I don't want it to happen. I don't want what's going to happen to happen. "Not like this," I burble through blood and spit.

Loudest thud of my life hits my ears. Then it's like all the sound gets sucked away. Then a giant whoosh sound and suddenly there's no more pressure on my neck. There's no pressure on my body at all.

I'm in the air.

And I'm getting higher and higher. Under me, the gendarmes are all frozen mid-fall, caught in the middle of a fireless, smokeless explosion. Meanwhile, something—someone—is carrying me higher into the sky.

Around me are figures cloaked all in black. I can barely tell them apart from the night sky. And they wear scarves just as dark all over their faces.

Just when I'm about to get my breath back, I see something that has me gasping for air. The person carrying me. Right along the left side of their stomach. Three stylized red lines. We're upside down in the air, getting higher and higher, when our eyes meet.

I'm looking at a Floater.

CHAPTER TWENTY-NINE

My legs are dangling, but my wrists are untied. I'm starting to resent the angle this Floater's holding me at. A sack of grain they haven't yet lifted on their shoulder. But the burning around my neck is just a memory and not the real thing, so I'm grateful.

I can't call what they're doing flying. More like stepping off of invisible stones in a river. Pushing off like gazelles or something. Sometimes, they'll run sideways along a wall or the façade of someone's home or they'll scale the height of an église. Graceful as all get-out. But there's always a dip as they leap to the next step, and I can't help but grunt when the arm holding me scrapes at an old wound. Old being anything between this morning and three years ago.

They don't settle on any surface for long. Be it someone's roof or the inner courtyard of a French estate or the disused train cars on the faraway, half-built rail lines. As we all head wherever we're heading, they start to split off until it's just the one carrying me and two others. The novelty of being carried through the air like this has started to wear off.

"Hey," I tell whoever's got my life in the crook of their arm. "Hey, let me down. Come on."

My carrier looks a little annoyed, but maybe that's just me projecting. I can't see their face all that well, covered up as it is and during the nighttime to boot. But eventually, we pass through what feels like an invisible wall, a borderline, and I know somewhere along that line is a checkpoint manned by gendarmes who have no idea what's going on a couple hundred meters away.

"They will know," says the Floater.

Ah, so they can read minds too.

"I know what you're wondering. I'd be wondering it too."

Once the rooftops get more recognizably dugu, we land on top of one midsize tower. It's broad and has some furniture and potted plants covered in netting. We land with the softest of taps. "How do you know what—"

The Floater puts a finger to their lips. "They're sleeping." They nod their head at the ladder that leads down into an interior courtyard for the living complex.

"Okay, never mind that." I lower my voice anyway. "You all work for Kadiatou?"

An impenetrable expression.

"Okay, work with Kadiatou." That softens the Floater up. "I have a message for her. It's urgent. It's impossible for me to communicate to you just how urgent this message is."

But the Floater just looks at me, doesn't say anything else.

"Take me to her!"

"We don't bang with that traitor."

"What?"

But then the Floater flips upside down and shoots feet-first into the sky. They're gone.

Weak-feet that I am, I should be grateful that they brought me this far and that they didn't leave me in hostile territory. Should also be grateful that they didn't drop me right out of the sky at any point since my rescue. But if the Murutilen gets a good evening from a mogofagala and I coulda stopped it but for this dramatic Floater, I'll probably be a bit upset.

Still, once I get my head on straight, it doesn't take me long to figure out where I am. After that, some step-retracing and some gettin' lucky, and I'm in a patch of darkened alley in front of what I'm gonna guess is a metal door. I knock the way I heard it the first time, and then a piece of metal slides open at eye level. The person on the other side sees me, then their eyes go wide. "Oh shit," I hear from the other side. The door scrapes open in fits and spurts. Hands grab me, greedy, and pull me into the headquarters.

It's all assistants and a few people I've never seen before crowded around me. Then I recognize one of the drummers. Takes me a second because I don't know what he looks like when he's not glaring.

"Kadiatou," I say to everyone. "I need to speak with Kadiatou right now."

They're still fussing over me, but down the hall stomps a familiar figure. "What on earth have you been doing out there?"

I break away from the group. "We gotta talk somewhere private."

She glances at the others, takes stock of the situation, then nods and leads me down another maze of hallways.

The door to this next room is an actual one, not just a beaded curtain.

"What is it?" she says once she locks the door. "And, Allah, what happened to your neck?" She's on me before I can push her off, examining it, pushing away shirt collar.

"That's not important." I get an elbow in the way and nudge her off. Much as it hurts to stop a woman from fussing over me. Much as I miss it. "Look, where's the Murutilen?"

She freezes. Frowns at me. "Why?"

"They're coming after him."

"Who's 'they'?"

"The people who don't want the world to find out about those mass graves. The people running this whole thing. That's who."

I'm getting loud, and I know it, but I can't stop. Even as I know I can get more done keeping my voice down, it all comes out as near shout anyway. "Where is he? We have to let him know so that—"

She grabs my arm with enough force to hold me still.

"What? What are you doing?"

"People have always been after him."

"Don't be stupid. I'm not talking about garden-variety government folk or a rival candidate or that stooge who's our current president." I lean in close. "These people have a mogofagala. Maybe more than one. Kadiatou, they're serious."

But she holds my stare.

Now I'm the one feeling stupid. Of course this is probably something they've considered since before they really had a reason to. Of course the guy would be a target. Of course people would try to get after him, people with different ways of getting that done. People with different hands on the different gears that make the world turn the way it does. They probably went through the possibility of a mogofagala being sent after him a long time ago. Hell, probably before I started chasing down leads trying to figure out what was killing dugulenw in the Ethnic Quarter.

"I appreciate your worry, but I need to know a little bit more about why you suddenly believe this is a problem."

Yeah, that'll probably help. Instead of me bursting in here like a bleeding lunatic, I could lay out just how I came across this bit of intelligence. Like someone who hasn't been Touched. Still, there might be stuff it's better for Kadiatou not to know the details of. Like the warehouse. "Friend of mine is involved in French society. She's a businesswoman. She had connections to a landowner, the guy we were talking about earlier: Honoré Mirbeau de L'Isle-Adam."

"Connections? What kind of connections?"

"Oh, they're not in business together or anything like that." I remember the way Aissata shot up the man's office. "They're more like competitors. Besides, you get to a certain level of rich and everyone knows everyone. At least, that's what I hear. I've never been rich before, so I wouldn't know. Anyway, it's him."

"Him what?"

"He's the guy building the French housing developments on the mass graves. Wants to keep it all hush-hush. And all of the Murutilen's talk of the Truth and Reconciliation Commission, well, he didn't take too kindly to all of that."

"He sounds like he's rich enough to buy his way out of any problems that come up. Why not just buy votes for his guy?"

This is where speculation comes in. This is where me punching above my weight comes in. Me sticking my head up above my pay grade. "The election needs to at least look aboveboard. I think the Murutilen's doing well enough that Honoré would wind up showing his hand no matter what he did. Or losing."

"But going after the Murutilen."

"It's his only way out. Only way of making absolutely sure his project doesn't get stopped."

Something I've said must have made an impression with Kadiatou. She lets go of my arm, then strokes her chin. "It would have to be in public."

"What do you mean? They'd go after the Murutilen in the middle of a crowd?"

"You have to understand. Someone like the Murutilen, to most people they seem bigger than us. The things that claim our lives, that restrict them, they seem to bounce off of people like the Murutilen. He's bigger than misfortune. Bigger than—"

"Death."

"That's the perception. And it needs to stay that way because we cannot ask the dugu to put all its hopes into a man."

"That's a dangerous game you're playing."

"When we win, people won't be talking about how dangerous it was. But killing him in public like that, it's a way of saying the State always wins. No matter how special your person, your candidate, your savior may be, the State always wins. Maybe we'll see the assassin. Maybe we won't. But that's likely how it'll happen."

"So at night he's safe?"

"At night, he's safe from the men with money. It's the diaro you have to worry about at night."

"So when's his next rally?"

"Tomorrow."

"Cancel it."

"What?"

"Are you mad? Cancel it. Tell him to call it off."

"You're joking. We can't just—"

The door lock clicks, and the door opens. A moment later, it shuts. The Murutilen is taller than me now that we're nearly face-to-face. And his smile is weird, looks pasted on, a little tired, and his eyes are thin. Almost closed. But him being there cuts Kadiatou off like a gendarme's sword.

"Your concern is greatly appreciated, Monsieur." He says it in that reedy voice I first heard that one afternoon in the crowd. "But I have no intention of canceling my next speech. Kadiatou, could you perhaps give us the room? I'd like to speak for a bit with my friend."

CHAPTER THIRTY

"How are you, my friend?"

"How the hell am I supposed to answer that question?"

"However you'd like."

"Where would I even begin? I . . . I've been beat up by dugu heavies, almost strangled to death by gendarmes, almost caught in a terrorist attack by I still don't know who, and it just feels like the deeper I get into this, the more them two halves of the world are ripping me apart."

". . ."

"Sounds like I should probably stop what I'm doing."

"It sounds like you've never said all of this out loud before."

"What?"

"When's the last time someone asked after you? Not simply to be polite or to adhere to custom. But with care and intention and curiosity. Genuine curiosity."

"I . . . I mean. Maybe Moussa? But you never know with policier. They'd ask the sky what color it is to chase a clue. I don't know. There's not really anyone in my life like that."

"Could be a proprietor. Someone who owns a tea shop you frequent or who stocks a cart you pass by every day in the souq. A neighbor who loans you their water source. But my asking that question is not meant to bring you pain. It is only to show you that, well, it can be helpful to say these things out loud. To say what you feel, how you feel, and why you are feeling it."

"Feelings get in the way in my line of work."

"Oh? And what do you do exactly?"

"I'm a chercher. I find missing people."

"Mmm."

"Most of the time, they're people that don't wanna be found. Sometimes, they're simply misplaced. A father forgets to pick up his child from school. Or someone misses a caravan back home and whoever pays me is convinced their cousin's been kidnapped. Sometimes it's that sort of thing. Most of the time, though, it's people hiding. They're on the lam, tryna get away from a bad situation. Or a situation they expect to be bad. Falling in love with the wrong person. Sometimes, it's a kidnapping. Those times, it feels good to be serving a higher purpose, you know? Feels like I'm doing some good. Contributing to . . . I dunno, things. But, yeah, that's my job."

"So you've had to spend quite a bit of time reading people, understanding them. What drives them, what drives them away."

"Yeah, you get pretty good at that. Even if your batting average isn't too hot."

"Batting average?"

"Never mind. I just mean that even if you're not good at the job, you get good at that part. Helps you figure out what jobs are worth taking and what aren't. If you're in a position to be picky, that is."

"Do you ever feel that you remain a mystery to yourself?"

"I . . ."

"Hmm?"

"Yeah. Guys like me, we're not exactly prone to introspection. Tough, ironic exterior makes it easier to move through a world where you're constantly running up against the worst of what we do to each other. The way the world is, making its mark on the way you are. Maybe you're born different or maybe you get your eyes opened when you're young and you just stay that way. Or go deeper into that end of the lake. You don't ask yourself questions about yourself because the answer's always simple."

"And yet . . ."

"Heh. And yet."

"Hmm. When I was young, my father passed. He was old. It was time. My mother was left a widow. She was the third wife, the most beloved. But she stood to inherit the least. So while my siblings grew fat off the inherited land, with varying degrees of success in their business ventures, my mother took me to the city back when it was just beginning. And she sought out work and I, her only son, assisted her in that work. Cleaning up after the French, making neat their homes and their offices, emptying their washbasins, sweeping, that sort of thing. One day, I asked her if she'd been happy, married to my fa. We were bagging up someone's refuse, preparing it for disposal. And she stopped. I remember. She was still hunched over and she remained that way for a long time. I thought that she hadn't heard me. But the truth is that she had never been asked that question before. She'd never had occasion to consider it. It was simply her portion to be married to my fa. She was wed to him while very young, younger than I was when I asked her that question. Being his wife had been her whole life. And it never occurred to her that happiness was part of the bargain. Maybe she had been happy and didn't know what to call it. Maybe not."

"She ever answer your question?"

"I do not remember her answer. I remember only her hesitation."

"Hmm. Did it screw you up? Her doing that?"

"I don't know. All I know is that I'm still not married. Maybe my bamuso has something to do with that."

"She still with us?"

"No, she died a long time ago."

"I hope she's happy."

"I hope so too."

"That why you got involved in politics? Seeing the French up close like that, being their janitor, you see something there that gave you the spark or whatever?"

"Maybe. It may be something deeper. Something having to do with having a say in your future. In how your life is to be lived."

"Getting out from under the French?"

"No. Living alongside them. Living with them. With my mother, I saw a great intermingling. I saw dugulenw servants in French homes. But I also saw dugulenw men of industry, wearing an admixture of French clothes and what you might find in the dugu. I saw children of mixed heritage holding their diéman mother's hand. I saw dugulenw and diéman smiling lovingly at each other. I saw dugulenw in the halls of power. I saw possibility. What I'm after, it isn't to throw off the yolk of colonialism. It's . . . it's a gift to my bamuso. That's what I'm after. Her entire life from childhood until death was dictated to her. Ruled by obligation. She was always serving someone, even when that someone was me. I would have liked to have seen her happy. Doing what she wanted. Doing a thing not because she needed to feed me or because her husband demanded it of her."

"Seems like it's all about the dames."

"Are you similarly organized?"

"I'm in this whole mess because a girl showed up at my apartment one night needing my help."

"And did you help her?"

"As much as I could. Didn't work in the end."

"She's no longer with us, I take it."

"No. She wound up floating in the air above the city square."

"Hmm."

"What do you think about all that? The floating. The magic. It's not strange to you?"

"Is it strange to you?"

"I . . . I didn't know it could happen like that."

"It didn't seem real?"

"No, it did. I knew exactly how real it was soon as I saw it. That wasn't my question. It wasn't 'how'd she end up like that' but more 'who did that to her,' you know? I thought it went away, you know, when all this business with the French started. Like, we were all ground-bound, you know? This is where life was gonna be lived. In the dirt. Floating like that, you go long enough without seeing it and you think it's a dream. You start to wonder if it was ever real to begin with. When I saw that girl strung up there like that, it brought it all back."

"You sound like the memories that returned to you weren't good ones."

" . . . "

"What did you do before you were a chercher?"

"I was in the sorodassi."

"You fought for the French, I take it."

"That's right."

"Why?"

"What?"

"Why did you join the sorodassi?"

" . . . "

"Another one of those questions you never thought to ask yourself. Or another one of those questions you've never been asked?"

"I try not to be too loud about my history. Closes off certain lines of work."

"I see."

"But I don't know why I did it. Chasing opportunity, I guess. I spent a lot of time between the two worlds. The dugu and the city. See, I'm deux-fois."

"I've not heard the term."

"Heh. It's . . . you know why they call people like me deux-fois? They probably call those little mixed kids you saw the same thing."

"Why do they use that term?"

"Because God had to try twice with us. The first time we came out, we came out all wrong. So He tried again but that just made us worse. So He gave up."

"Hmm."

"Yeah. So I bounced back and forth between the dugu and the city. The dugu was my bamuso's home. Where she came from. And my fa, he's français."

" . . . "

"No, I never got to ask her if she was happy either."

"Well, at least I know I'm not alone in making that mistake. Did you ever feel like you were confused growing up? Lacked any sense of belonging?"

"No. The opposite, really. Felt like whatever I wanted, I could take. I know that's a very français way of thinking, but that's just how I felt as a kid. Join the sorodassi when called, get that tuition discount for school, maybe become an avocat or something."

"But it didn't turn out that way."

"You know what happened during the wars. Didn't turn out that way for a lot of us. Plenty of folks got rich off of it. But the rest of us . . . well, my best friend in the sorodassi, he's a policier. I used to needle him about it too. But that confusion you were talking about, that didn't happen till later in life."

"Where are you now?"

"I don't really have a place to sleep right now. The military took over my home and my office. It's one of their bases now for whenever they wanna raid the Ethnic Quarter."

"But that's where you've been living? The Ethnic Quarter?"

"Since I left school, yeah."

"Why?"

"I dunno. Guilt? I think . . . I think I was hoping someone would find me out, you know? I couldn't tell anyone what happened in the sorodassi, but maybe if I hung around enough, someone would recognize me and there'd be some sort of . . . I dunno, a reckoning?"

"You wanted absolution."

"Penance, yeah. Absolution, maybe. I think I wanted to be punished."

"Being a chercher is dangerous?"

"It's how I got most of my scars, yeah."

"So you made a punishment for yourself."

"You could say that, yeah."

"What do you think of the Truth and Reconciliation Commission I plan on bringing about?"

"I guess you could say I'm agnostic."

"You're not worried about what may come out about you? What you've done?"

"You know what? A big chunk of me doesn't actually think it's going to happen. I've lived this long without anyone holding me accountable, holding any of us accountable mostly. Why would that change?"

"That's not exactly true."

"What?"

"That no one's been held accountable."

"I don't follow."

"Well, the attacks on retired members of the sorodassi. The

bombings. The jatigewalekela campaign. That's accountability of a sort."

"Guess I kept a low enough profile that I dodged those bullets."

"Bullets, indeed."

"But, yeah, you're right. Some of my fellows, they aren't exactly in one piece right now. I don't envy them, though. I don't look at 'em and think they got lucky getting their house blown up or getting their family clapped or anything like that. It ain't like that. I know it's some combination of luck and self-preservation that's kept me whole so far, as stupid as I get sometimes. Feels like that's changing, though."

"With this case."

"Yeah. That girl. She changed things for me." She was my reckoning. For what I'd done. For thinking being deux-fois made me français, made it so I could act like them, be like them. Be evil like them. I made her, and she was the bill come due. But because I'm a man and a mystery to myself and my job means I'm not supposed to give this much of myself to strangers, I just say, "Guess she's why I'm sitting here talking to you right now like this."

"Trying to save my life."

"Yeah. Trying to save your life."

"You know you can't save my life."

" . . ."

"I will die doing what I'm trying to do. I made my peace with that a long time ago. And some of my people, they've made their peace as well. Many will mourn me when it happens. But I can't do what I need to do if I think I'll live long enough to see it through. Sometimes, it's enough to hope that someone will come after me to carry on the work."

"You think I'm that somebody?"

"No, not at all! That's not what I meant. Allah, that's funny. No, no, not at all."

"I'm gonna assume there's no insult in all that."

"Oh, you're fine. Allah, I haven't laughed like that in too long. Thank you, friend. But I mean only to say that what I'm doing—what we are all doing—is bigger than me."

"Yeah, that's the vibe I'm getting from your people. I saw how you moved that crowd too."

"Then you know how important this work is. Of course, the government is going to try to stop me. There are no lengths to which they won't go. Even if it means attacking their own."

"What?"

"You wondered who was responsible for the attack on the French Quarter."

"You're saying the French did that to themselves?"

". . ."

"Where'd you get that?"

"It's some of the munitions that were used in the bombing."

"That . . . that's an organ."

"Sealed and preserved, yes. This is what the Floaters carve out of their body. When deployed in a certain way, it becomes an explosive device. You saw the result of the bombing."

"Yeah, the raids and the cordoning off of the Ethnic Quarter."

"The government conducted the bombing as a pretext to barricade the dugulenw until after the election. Their justification: keep election-related violence at a minimum. They claim they are doing this to maintain the peace."

"They bombed their own." Kadiatou had told me that the jatigewalekela weren't responsible for the bombing. They'd done other things but not that. The français . . . they knew what those organs did. And they bombed their own people. Did they carve up all those dugu the kid was telling me about too? Were français really behind those killings? Honoré's goons? Cutting up dugu-lenw just so they could blow up their own people? It's that terror Moussa told me about, how the difference between horror and terror is that terror's a violation of the world. It's what the horror you see is tellin' you about horror you haven't seen yet. The horror you can't see even when you're staring it in its white face. Even if they didn't put the knife to her stomach, the French killed that girl.

"Yes," he says, and it's like he's answering every question I ever had. Like he knows it all too. And it's enough to unclench my fists. It's enough to bring him back into focus. "They have to resort to subterfuge because if they were to openly try stopping our movement, the people would revolt. The result wouldn't be scattered jatigewalekela attacks. It wouldn't be targeted killings. The result would see the city burn down."

"Why are you giving this to me?"

He's silent.

"This is what you're up against."

"I know."

"But . . ."

"The thing I'm fighting . . . it's the isolation. You know what happens when a place gets big enough. People stop knowing each other. It's like a muscle, belonging to a community. If you leave it for too long, it atrophies. You forget you were ever able to greet your neighbor. The world is filled with strangers forever closed off to you. They have replaced human beings you once had it in you to learn. To love. We cannot remove the French. They will remain here as long as there are things here for them to covet. I'm talking about our survival. How do we stay alive long enough to make sure our children are safe and able to live lives of their own choosing? I do not condone violence, but I will not condemn my people. Our people. I am able to do what I am doing because they did what they did. But what violence does, it closes you off, it turns the world into a stranger. Into worse than that. Something unknowable and impossible to know, something easy to kill. Surely you've seen enough killing in your life. Help me move us past it."

"How? What can I do?"

". . ."

"You're smiling, and I got no idea what it means."

"You will."

"You're gonna have to do better than that, chief. This whole case, people been talking to me in riddles all cryptic-like, and just when I think I've figured it out and gotten out the other end of the tunnel, I look up and it's just more tunnel. I figured out the thing I started this whole thing trying to figure out and it just all feels unfinished. No closure. And, sure, that's an occupational hazard. My line of work, there's rarely a clear-cut ending. It's more ragged. The question is 'where is this person' and the answer is rarely satisfying, but there's an answer. And it didn't used to matter to me because I got paid and the person paying me got their answer. But there's no end here, is there? I know what that girl was after, but I don't feel like I've solved shit. I—"

"You're lost."

"Hell yeah, I'm lost. More lost than I've ever been in my damn life."

"I don't have the answer you're looking for."

"Answer? I don't even know what question I'm asking anymore."

"But you're still asking it. That is the important part. That is always the most important part."

CHAPTER THIRTY-ONE

And that's where we left it.

This time when I make my way through the crowd, people are smiling at me. That's the mood. Ebullient. These people can't be touched. They've already won. Nobody's trying to block my way. I'm sure if I saw that doctor again that I was chasing through here last time, he'd smile and clap me on the shoulder. And I'd let him. This type of weather, with the breeze like this and the sun like that and the sky like this, very hard to keep a grudge. This ain't weather to chase anybody in.

Looking at the Murutilen on stage now, talking like everybody in front of him's a long-lost family member or a cousin he hasn't seen in years, power isn't the first thing that comes to mind. But you can't ask for better weather, and, having spent so long in a room with him, I got the sneaking suspicion that he had a hand in it. Could call the sun out from behind the clouds if he wanted. And he deigned to spend a whole night chatting me up about my life, my directionless, isolated, curmudgeon ass.

You don't think a man with a voice like that could command an army, but today's the first day the government lifted the curfew and the barricades went down. First day a lot of us are walking down these city streets again, and it's a swarm. I can imagine someone somewhere high in a tower looking down on the teeming mass below and nudging their impressionable children behind their skirts. Running for cover in the face of an advancing army. But that's not what these dugulenw are who've spilled out of the Ethnic Quarter. Nothing army about the cowrie-shell necklaces or the bangles or the line dances. Nothing army about the singing and the chants and the flowers the kids pin in the belts of the ofisiden ye manning the voting booths. It's all joy. And if you were to ask them who made it happen, they wouldn't point to the sun, they wouldn't point to the sky. They'd point at that stage. All of them. They'd point right at that stage, and they wouldn't be wrong.

Throughout the crowd, a few folks note the skylines, squint at rooftops. His protection detail looking for threats. Whether or not it could happen today, now, it's still up in the air. So far, everyone—Kadiatou, me, the Murutilen—we're all just guessing on what the other side's gonna do. I don't even know if he had his food checked last night. Might not be a shot from a hand cannon that does it. Might not be a knife. Might just be bad stew. I'm hoping my bad-luck orbit has started wearing off by now.

People have started climbing up walls and sitting on the roofs of the lower buildings. Shebab hang from pegs sticking out of the Mize's main tower. You wouldn't know that the remains of the French Quarter are just past the wall of rubble behind the Mize.

I make my way to a higher vantage point, and up here on this bit of walkway running along one side of the square, you really get a sense of just how many people are showing up for this. The streets are choked with people. There's some muscling about, but it's that playful kind of rowdy, not the mean kind. Every argument ends with cheek-kisses today.

Can't help looking into some of the windows of the nearby towers and apartment buildings, looking for people I might know. Maybe Aissata's somewhere around here keeping an eye on things. I know she must've gotten out of that shoot-out scot-free. I should thank her next time I see her. Maybe Moussa's somewhere here too. Can't remember the last time I saw him. Had to have been less than a week ago, but it feels like a couple lifetimes have passed since I last heard him joke about my belly. Since I last smelled that odor of français that always hung about him. If I had one on me, I'd light it up just to be reminded of him.

This far away, I can't hear the Murutilen speak. I can barely hear the drumming. But somehow everybody knows when to go quiet. Like a wave passing over the whole crowd. We all get the same signal. And I hear the faintest whisper of vowels and consonants, but mostly I hear birdsong. When's the last time I heard birdsong?

While his speech is going on, I check the shadowed alleys for any movement, any glint of light off a partially sheathed sword. Any official persons moving into position. An old habit, testing the air for the change. Scenting it for trouble. For blood. I know I'm not the only one out here waiting for the other shoe to drop.

From one angle, this has gotta look like provocation. If they don't already know, then all most people here need to do is shuffle a little ways north to see that a good chunk of where diéman used to live still hangs in the air. In fact, with most of it having fallen from the sky, those bits of house and body still floating look all the more disquieting. Even more like some natural law's been broken. We already paid for it once with the riot, and we paid for it again with the lockdowns. Some folks down there, if not them, then people they knew, paid a couple times over. And who knows if some poor dugulenw still aren't paying for it in a kaso cell somewhere, forgotten? But that isn't to say that those on the other side of it think the ledger's been balanced. I know enough about loans and interest payments, debts and credit, to know that it's usually up to only one side when the whole thing is settled. You could bring a debt collector every dime they're asking for. They'd still find a way to bleed you for more. So that's what I'm on the lookout for. Debt collection. Some français saying, okay we let you have this man, let you put your hope for a new future in him, we let you have the damn birds singing, now it's time to pay up.

Never used to feel so us-versus-them about things, but maybe that's the clarity that's come with going so far down this path, swimming this deep into the watering hole. You go out past where the shore dips and discover there's a lot more underneath you than you thought. You don't know how deep it goes. Trying to find out on your own will get you killed. But at least you know. So even as my insides are more confused than ever, the world's got a sharpness to it that it didn't used to have. The silhouettes of bodies and buildings are more defined, bolder. The sky's color is more intense. The different scents of the city, the shisha flavors. I can pick them apart better now. I can see things for how they really are.

Also feels like I finally picked a side.

I thought it'd feel like I lost something if the moment ever came. Like I was giving up some magic ability to move between worlds. Like my face was a set of identity papers that could get me through whatever invisible or visible checkpoints divided the dugu from the city. I could go where the dugulenw were kept out, and I could go where the diéman would be looked at funny. I could go in and pick up whatever it was I was looking for. And all I ever wanted was what could serve me. What could solve a case, really, but that was it. Damn this man speaking right now for getting me to dream a bit bigger.

I'm laughing to myself when something brushes up against me and I look down at my right flank to find the urchin perched right next to me, peering out at the stage the Murutilen's standing on. I'm a long time looking at him, searching him for bruises or scrapes or anything that'll tell me some of what he's been through since we last saw each other. But he looks just the same. Maybe a bit of bruising around the collarbone from when one of Kadiatou's guards practically hoisted the kid in the air on the walk from Zoe's. But other than that, he's the same kid that promised to steal me property records just a couple days ago. In fact, he looks cleaner. More put together. Fewer holes in his shirt. A little bit less dirt about the ankles. Smells cleaner too. Not that I'm one to judge.

I don't say anything to the kid. He woulda announced himself to me out loud if he'd wanted. Instead, I tousle his hair a little bit. He bats me away but he does it like he secretly wants me to keep going.

But when he brushed against me, I felt the weight of what was in my pocket, and I'm reminded of all of last night. One way to keep the other shoe from dropping is to move the ground.

"Hey, kid," I say without looking at the urchin. "Come with me. I wanna show you something."

CHAPTER THIRTY-TWO

During our walk, the urchin somehow winds up with three apples in his hands. Never saw him pay. But I don't see any shop-keepers chase after him either. Been a while since I seen hands that good.

He doesn't ask where we're going. Just juggles the apples while we walk. Or tries to. A couple times, he almost drops them, all gangly limbs and whatnot. And just when he falls into a rhythm, he bumps into someone trying to buy jewelry or suya and almost loses the whole batch to the dirt. Before he's even got a chance to get angry, he's back at it. I wonder if Moussa's ever looked at his kids the way I'm looking at this one. A little bit of admiration with a healthy dose of wonder, a sprinkling of appreciation at the kid's ability to lose himself in something so innocuous, all stirred together in a stew and heated over a pot. Makes me wanna do everything in my power to protect the kid. Keep him from heartbreak, go after anyone who'd even think of putting a finger on him. Don't know whether Moussa would call me soft or slap me on the back and smile his approval.

When we get to a ladder running up a brickmaker's factory, I send him up first and cover the rear. "Go all the way up," I tell him. "To the roof. I wanna see something."

He pockets the apples, including the one he'd been eating, raises an eyebrow at me, then up he goes. I follow.

We get all the way to the top and the streets have thinned out a little bit. Traffic's a bit more manageable. You can even see donkey carts moving through. On the way up, I worried that the view wouldn't be as good as the one Kadiatou showed me, but that worry gets dashed away once we get to the edge. We have to swat our way through some laundry to get there. But it's all laid out in front of us.

"What am I looking at?" the kid asks me. He's got the apple out again.

I point far past the outskirts. We're in the outer arrondissements but there are still small settlements, really just shacks and tiny collections of scraped-together homes beyond that. Then there's a stretch of savannah, then desert, then a housing development. "See that?"

He's still munching his apple. But I can tell now that the whole nonchalance he's got going about him is an act. Maybe he's remembering the last time we were up on high ground looking at one of these things. He's remembering what I musta looked like, how it musta felt standing next to me when I got like that. Probably remembering what I did afterward. Shame hits me like a stake through the chest. What's done is done. Can't take it back. And, besides, this time is different. My head's clear. I know exactly what I'm doing. "Yeah, I see it. What about it?"

"From here, can you see if there are people around?"

He tosses the apple core and steps a little closer to the edge. I'd be worried about him if I didn't already know how comfortable he was on the city's rooftops. He squints. Then he inches forward and shades his eyes. Looks to the left, pans right and back.

There's a moment where even I get a little anxious. He's practically gripping the roof's edge with his toes. And those sandals don't look like they got the best grip in the world. Then he backs off with a little hop.

"Nope," he says. "Didn't see anybody."

"What about inside the homes?"

He shakes his head. "Not even guards. But the place isn't finished yet, so why would there be people in it?"

"Just checking." I put my hand to the part of my pocket where the package bulges a little. "I want your help with a thing. Feel free to say no. You got every right. And I can't promise any payment. This isn't a thief job. But we're gonna sneak into that development."

"And do what?" When I don't answer, he arches an eyebrow at me. "And do what? What's over there?"

"Look, kid. I'm mixed up in something big here. Bigger than I ever thought. And I'm in the middle of a really deep lake just trying to swim to the other side. A lot's changed for me since I started this case. You could say I finished it, but it doesn't feel finished. Not by a long shot. There's some stuff I gotta make right. Some stuff from before. Stuff I thought I'd left behind, really. But it turns out that you can build on top of bones all you want, they're still gonna be there. There's been a lot of darkness. Darkness came after me that one night, and I been living in it for a long time even before then. But I got a chance to shine some light. And if that brings me closer to the other side of the lake, then I'm gonna chase that chance. I've tried to keep the hurt close to me, but some folks been dragged up in it and punished because of me. Can't help but feel responsible for that. And that's on me. Which is why I'm asking you and not tryna trick you into doing anything you don't wanna do."

For a long time, he's silent. Just has that quizzical expression on his face. "We breakin' the law or something?"

"Technically, yes." I fold my arms. "That gonna be a problem?"

"Nope. Do I need to bring any of the others? How big is this job?"

"Just you and me."

"Sounds dangerous." He shrugs. "Probably just as well. They'd never work for free. Me, I'm the sap."

"Any further questions?"

"We got time to eat? I'm starving."

I can feel my face loosen. "Sorry, kid. I don't got any money. I'm pinched. And I can't really go back home either. Not that there'd be any change to scrounge up. I don't even have cushions for the coins to hide under."

"I can pay this time."

"What?"

"Yeah. You think just 'cause you can't get work that the rest of us are busy being bums? I don't know who you told about the Mize job, but, hey, things have picked up. The crew's happy. Consider this a payment for your recommendation."

I don't know what I did or who the kid thinks I musta talked to, but I just say thank you.

It's not till it's gotten dark and we're finishing our beans and tatale that I get the sneaking suspicion that there was no recommendation. It's just the kid being generous.

We get some extra water when we leave. Even though the trek out to the development didn't look that far from the rooftop, we don't have a cart and there's no straight path there yet. At least, not one that's been all the way constructed. So I don't know how long we'll be out there.

But something in the kid changes once we get within the boundaries of the planned community. He gets a bit more intentional. Hunches forward a little bit, kinda crouches. He's ready to work.

First, we skirt the perimeter, take note of the tree placement, where some have gone up and where the ground's been marked for others. Pretty easy pattern to figure out. While we're doing this, we check out the apartment buildings. They're all pretty much half constructed, so we can get a good look inside at the different floors and where walls have gone up to separate the rooms. A part of me wonders what the kid's thinking, looking at this. I don't know if this is his first glimpse at how the French might live or whether his work's brought him inside their homes before. Maybe he's had to steal things from rich diéman before. Maybe he's had to steal things for them. But when we look into the buildings, there's also something else I'm searching for. I'm making sure none of these are spots someone could come back to. Maybe they've set up something here and are just waiting in the city with friends or a cousin until the rest of their house is complete. As determined as I am about what I'm here to do, the thought of destroying the beginnings of someone's life here still twists me up. But the coast is clear.

Then we make our way to the center around which the community's being built. There's space for a fountain, and some of the building materials lie in sacks around it. But in the middle is a giant hole in the ground. I couldn't have asked for a more perfect spot. I just hope it matches my memory of the place.

At the hole's edge, I crouch and toss a small stone in and wait. Four seconds. That's how long it took to hit the bottom. Didn't sound like it smacked against wood on the way down either.

Then I gather some rope and knot it around my waist.

"Here," I tell the kid, handing him the other end. "Brace yourself against that sack there. Make sure it's secure. Yeah, tie it like that." I tug his knot a little tighter. "I'm going in."

I only give myself permission for a few breaths before I climb down. The walls of the hole are close enough that I can steady myself without spreading my arms all the way out. Still, not being able to see the bottom shakes me up a bit.

Eventually, my feet stop. My knees almost buckle when I hit the bottom. But I stomp just for good measure. Still secure.

That's when I pull the package out of my pocket. I know the organ's been out of body for some time now, but I can't convince myself it doesn't still feel warm in my hand. Still greasy, still fresh. I wanna let it go, but I can't.

"C'mon, man. Just do it." I squeeze my eyes shut, and the first thing I see is the girl. Her face. Those eyes, looking straight through me. When they're open again, I got a new peace about me. So I'm not shaking when I scrape out a little opening at the base of the hole with my foot and slide the organ in. And I'm not shaking when I find a sharp little stone and make a quick incision width-wise. Gas hisses out.

I tug the rope twice, then three times. And with a little help from the kid, I make my way back up.

"All right. Untie it, quick. Let's get out of here."

"We done?" he asks as we make a break for the desert.

"Just keep running."

We're still running when we feel the rumble. Then the explosion—stronger than I expected—throws us forward. I scramble to my feet and am about to take off again when I see the kid's still on the ground. He's turned around and resting on one elbow.

"Hey. Kid. Get up." I get down next to him, ready to pick him up. "Hey, you all right? Anything broken?" And I'm about to gather him up in my arms when I follow his gaze and see what he's staring at. Moonlight cuts through so you can see some of the shapes hovering in the air. And if you look long enough, you can tell it's all organized like a sphere. It's mostly clods of dirt and chunks of recently laid stone, some trees hanging sideways or upside down. But if I got it right, then there should be other stuff mixed in. Stuff it might be too dark to see here, like this.

But stuff that might better reveal itself in the light. "C'mon, kid. Let's get out of here."

This time, he gets up on his own. No worse for wear. And we head back to the city. Already, lights have come on in some of the homes outside the outer arrondissements.

CHAPTER THIRTY-THREE

They're easier to see in the day, but you still have to squint. You're looking into the sunlight, kind of, so you have to shade your eyes, but squint hard enough, focus, and you'll see it.

You'll see the bones.

That revelation ripples through the whole crowd gathered. I make sure to hang back. It's been where I've stood all morning. The urchin still hasn't come back. But the first people to see it were some of the folks in the encampments on that strip of savannah at the desert's edge. You could see the thing from far enough away that they knew strangeness the second they laid their eyes on it. So they ran and got their neighbors. And other people who didn't see it right away got called and others made relays to the arrondissements and deeper into the city until everybody had crowded out to see that what had happened in the French Quarter has happened again.

The mood's different this time around. I think the eruption being farther away from people has something to do with it. It's less terrifying when it's not happening just around the corner. People point, just as you expect they would. They gawk, just as you expect they would. A few faint, there are a couple shocked exclamations to the higher being. But mostly it's hushed whispers, like they don't want that higher being to hear their speculation. Like this is supposed to be a mystery, not a revelation.

But then they start to see the bones.

I hear one person whisper that they were right, there were

people killed in the explosion. This is another attack just like what happened to those français in the French Quarter. Another nods her head in agreement. A third asks when the diéman started moving in here and a fourth chimes in that they didn't even know this place was here, last they checked, it was all bad farmland. You couldn't grow a single groundnut in this soil.

The urchin's still nowhere to be found. I hope he isn't feeling guilty or anything like that. He might think we killed someone, and I just wanna find him and tell him he did nothing wrong. Wanna wrap an arm around the kid's shoulder, pull him close, and tell him he's guilty of nothing. Absolutely nothing. Then I feel like shit because I asked him along when, thinking about it now, I coulda done the whole job myself. I think I just needed a witness. Not an accomplice, not someone to implicate or get caught up in a bad thing. But someone who could just see me perform my penance. I wanted to get caught doing a good thing, and he was the only one I could think to bring. Or maybe he thinks he'll get caught. Would probably tell me only stupid criminals return to the scene of the crime. But then I'd tell him something I learned from years of being a chercher. There's a little stupid in every criminal. Certainly in this one.

It isn't much longer before the first wave of gendarmes comes storming from the savannah. Clad in their metal with their hand cannons clanking at their sides, they look out of place among all that scrub. All that open land. Like an invading force.

I'm toward the back of the crowd so I and everyone around me scatter like we're supposed to. But up ahead, not everybody moves. Some of them don't even turn around. Instead, they've inched closer to the eruption. More curious about this thing than they are scared of the authorities. The batons come out and a few people get beat out of the way. But when the next wave comes with their cannons already out and aimed, circling the still-growing crowd, I wait for that electric fear to fill the air. The same charge that crackled on the skin the first time this happened. But that's not what happens. The dugulenw start shouting back.

They don't even bother speaking French. They shout and command and argue the way they would with anyone holding up the line outside their stall or like someone knocked over their water pot or bumped into them too roughly in the souq. Now it's the gendarmes on the back foot.

I don't believe what I'm seeing at first. It's like watching a city wake up from a dream. The monster's a lot smaller in the light.

Then I see another wave of people crest the hill and swarm the savannah. It's a sea of diéman. But they're not the raging torrent they were last time. They're more tentative. Some of them are already weeping. I'm torn up a bit, because I know some of them maybe lost someone in the last attack and they see something of a mirror here. Maybe they were expecting a relative to arrive, said this was where he was gonna be living, and now look at it. Maybe it's just too many strangenesses in a land already filled with people who don't look like them.

Almost all at once, the dugulenw turn to the just-arrived français, and there's that electricity I was waiting for. That flint-striking. I can practically hear the sparks leaping. The tinder's all here. I didn't set out to start a riot, but if that's what it comes to, then that's another thing I gotta bear on my conscience. Put it on my tab. The dugulenw look ready to rumble. Not like they're out for revenge. More like they're ready to defend themselves. And if, during the ensuing knuckle-up, some scores get settled, then so be it. I can practically hear the dugulenw saying, as one, you don't have enough cells in your kaso to lock us all up. That's what every one of 'em's saying with their eyes: your kaso ain't big enough for all of us.

"Murutilen!"

Takes me a second to realize that I'm the one that shouted that. Top of my lungs, too. Fist up in the air and all. What the hell is wrong with me?

"Murutilen!" It's a single shout from somewhere in the crowd behind me. Followed by ten more. Then ten more. The chant pulses through the crowd until it becomes a roar.

Murutilen! Murutilen! Murutilen!

I'm glad the urchin isn't with me, 'cause right now it's gotta be a thousand dugulenw behind me and several hundred diéman ahead and the only thing separating us is a strip of dirt about twenty meters wide. Gendarmes fill that space in a line, doing their best to look stone-faced, but it doesn't stop us. It only makes us louder.

Murutilen! Murutilen! Murutilen!

The ground's shaking with it. The diéman on the other side of the divide are feeling it too. They start to bare their teeth. Peel back their skin to reveal what they really want to do to us. But we get louder still.

Murutilen! Murutilen! Murutilen!

I'm glad the kid's not gonna get caught up in what's about to happen. He can hear about it later in the safety of whatever nook he's turned into a home in the Ethnic Quarter. Hear about how a bummy chercher with no money and barely a change of clothes threw down against the diéman with half the Ethnic Quarter at his back.

As one, the dugulen vanguard steps forward.

They'll sing songs about me, kid.

Another step forward. The gendarmes can smell my breath.

Another step.

We pump our fists with each shout.
Murutilen!
Murutilen!
Muruti—

CHAPTER THIRTY-FOUR

"Are you mad? I'm serious. Because this is deeper than anything I could have ever imagined. There is no hospital or temple in this city with the doctors you need. I swear not even the dugu chanteur could treat you. You are beyond help. Are you trying to kill me? Is that what you're trying to do? Are you trying to get me killed?"

I knew it sounded like Moussa. When I'm finally able to open my eyes all the way, I get a small shock of pride. Still able to tell dream from reality. But my mouth feels like it's been filled with desert, and my head feels like it got put under a donkey cart for about a kilometer.

"Get up." He smacks me with something hard. "I said get up!"

I trust the wall's still gonna be there when I sit up, and, yup, there it is. It's too bright in here. Then I check the angle of the light, the color of the dirt it's bouncing off of.

I'm in a kaso cell. Again.

"So you're the one who hit me." Takes a second, but my vision clears. He's leaning on a cane. That must be what he got me with.

"I only caught you the once. And that was to save your life."

"Very Moussa way of returning the favor."

His lips peel back in a snarl. "You and your shit-ass jokes, Bouba, I shoulda let you get torn apart."

I can't remember the last time I saw him this angry. "So what happened? Was there a riot?"

"Was that what you were after?"

I tell him no, and I don't know if I'm lying or not. To be honest, I have no idea what I was after. "Eyes and heart, Moussa, don't really know what I was thinking. Just got caught in the moment. Seeing another eruption like that, messes you up."

"Oh, is that right? Messes you up?" Then he's in my face. "What happened to 'find out who killed that girl,' huh? What happened to 'figure out who's killing all these dugulenw in the Ethnic Quarter, slicing them up and taking out their organs,' hmm? What happened to all that? I sent you in to solve some murders for me and now you're out here starting riots? Is this part of your plan? Is this your MO now? You change shit up on me since I last saw you work or have you just lost your touch?"

"I resent that implication, Moussa" is all I say, because I want nothing more than for him to get his hot breath out of my nose.

Like a charm, he backs off. He starts pacing. With that cane now part of his routine, it adds an unsettling click to his movements. Never thought it'd actually hurt seeing my friend with an infirmity. He starts muttering under his breath. Nothing important, just more of his frustration with me. But seeing and hearing him like this after so long wondering how he was doing, a lot of that fervor from earlier falls away. It was pretty selfish of me, the whole thing. But it did get me and Moussa in a room together. Still, I don't like him worrying over me like this. It don't become him, is, I guess, how I feel about it.

"I don't know whether you're gonna believe me or not, man, and frankly at this point I don't really care, but following the trail is exactly what I'm doing."

"So did you figure it out yet? You know who's killing these dugulenw?"

I stare hard at him. Trying to say without saying out loud "you may not wanna hear this answer."

He gets a sense of that, which is mission accomplished in a sense, but he still looks like he wants an answer. "Or are you still looking?" Which lets me off the hook. Very gracious of him.

"First time we really talked about the case, you hinted at there being . . . bigger elements involved."

"I hinted at there being other français involved."

"That ain't the same thing?" Time to clear the fog once and for all. "I think you were trying to misdirect me."

And now he looks like he got caught off guard. Caught with his hands down right in the left temple. Staggers him a bit. Damn near almost falls off his cane. "What are you talking about?"

"You wanted me to go looking for a diéman killer. But I think you wouldn't have been surprised if I never found one. You mighta pretended to be, but you never woulda made a good griot."

"What are you saying?"

"You know what a chasse au dahu is, Moussa?"

"Oh, brother. Another damn rabbit trail. Okay, go on. Tell me. What the hell is a chasse au dahu?"

"Well, the dahu's sorta like a mountain goat. Got the horns in the front, not as big as an ibex. Smaller. Cuter. Got stripes along the eyes right to its nose like this. Now, because they live on the mountains, they got this weird thing about them where the legs on one side are shorter than the legs on the other. Makes it easier to hop up and down them rocky mountains, I guess. But it also means they can only go around the mountain in one direction. Takes two people to catch one of these bad boys. You need someone with a bag, and someone who's good at imitating the dahu noises. Someone who knows what a dahu sounds like."

"Yeah? And what does a dahu sound like?"

"The idea's that the one with the bag stands at the bottom of the mountain slope. And the one making the dahu sounds surprises the animal from behind. Startles it, it falls over, rolls right into the bag. Sometimes, though, you gotta go higher up into the mountains. Wait all night for this thing. 'Cause, you know, it doesn't like to get caught."

"Go on with your story. How does this tie back to what we've been talking about?"

"You wanted me out there holding the bag. Dahu doesn't exist. It's fake. It's a practical joke the French play on each other. It's how kids trick their gullible friends into getting lost in the mountains. You wanted me out there lost and holding the bag while you did what? Got to the bottom of what's really going on? Be real with me just for one second, Moussa. You've been using me this whole time." I catch myself frowning at him. "Why? What were you trying to point me toward?"

Moussa's trembling with anger. "A suspect. A damn suspect. You always gotta look for what isn't there. You're seeing ghosts. And it's led you all the way here, doing what's gotta be the stupidest thing in the history of stupid things you've done. Since when did you ever care about politics anyway?"

"There's more than one of us inside of us, Moussa." Don't know where that came from. Sounded more profound in my head.

"You really are ill. You know what happens if that Murutilen guy or whatever the hell they call him wins the election? Actually wins the election? Do you? Are you aware of what happens? To us?"

I know what he's gonna say. And I know it's gonna tax him to say it out loud, but I'm angry at him and want the taxman to bleed him dry.

"It means that Truth and Reconciliation Commission happens. It means war crimes get investigated. It means everything the sorodassi did, under a microscope. Are you listening to me?

That's us. Me and you. All of us. Everything we did. Hey! Listen to me. What you're doing, what you are doing, it's gonna get us hanged. Do you hear me? Strung up. There won't be any immunity. No forgiveness. No amnesty or any of that shit. Not for us. Not even being deux-fois is gonna save you. You know what you'll be when all that shit goes down? A race-traitor. A damn race-traitor. On both sides. You hear me? You're damned twice. That's what happens if this guy wins the election."

Then it hits me. "You're the one who put those cops on election detail. That order didn't come from above you. That's you making sure your guy wins."

"Our guy, Boubacar. Our guy."

I shake my head and just barely keep from regretting it. Still hurts. I don't know why it shocks me that Moussa's this far gone. That he's this zealous about the pro-government candidate taking the throne. Moussa's policier. He is the government. Me, on the outskirts, being a chercher, not taking a regular salary from the français, there's always the risk someone like that is disloyal. But Moussa feeding his kids depends on just that loyalty. Moussa being a man depends on just that sort of loyalty. Maybe he really was a true believer when we were in the sorodassi. Maybe I was the fake.

"Drop this now, Bouba. For both our sakes. Just . . . just go home."

"I can't. Cops took it over and kicked me out."

CHAPTER THIRTY-FIVE

Zoe's is filled to bursting when I walk past.

The afternoon crowd has spilled out in front of the place. What used to be a few single regulars nursing their pipes during the lunch break or some old-timers who were practically one with the furniture all year round has turned into basically a party. If the party were serious, no one was laughing, and everyone was hunched over talking like they were engaged in conspiracy, not kids vandalizing but jatigewalekela planning some targeted mayhem.

Doesn't look like a place where I'm welcome. I can't tell what Zoe sees when she looks at me, probably because she hasn't looked at me in what feels like a long while. I'm getting a little concerned, though. Apolitical businesses where people go just to have fun, those places don't catch the government's eye. Those places don't get raided or shut down. But Zoe's looks more and more like the home base of a political party. Looks, right now, like the home base of the Murutilen's political party. Looks like the type of place gendarmes and the Red-and-Blacks would love to tear to pieces. This is what I was afraid of when it first came to me that Zoe was mixed up in all this stuff. Donating to political campaigns and all that. Is whatever you're looking for worth what's gonna happen if you keep this up? That's what I wanna ask her. I'd be minus a tooth before I finished the question, that's for sure.

"OH! LOOK WHO IT IS!" Someone out front is shouting

and pointing at me. It's a mess of djellabas and agbadas and beards. But it's a woman in a bògòlanfini blouse and wrapper set, who's up on her feet and making sure everyone for several side streets knows who I am. "HAI! IT'S THE GÈLÈYA DONBAGA. EVERYONE! OUR TROUBLEMAKER IS HERE!" Then, as one, everyone outside erupts in cheers. She grabs my sleeve and pulls me into a mass of people that swallows me whole in a sandstorm of back slaps and "AYE, MY BROTHER!" and "THEY COULD NEVER KEEP YOU CAGED" plus cup after cup of palm wine shoved into my hands.

I get passed along and slapped and caressed and plied with drink until they set me in a seat in what must be the premium spot where the high rollers get to sit in the place. The cushions feel like they got that high thread count. Even the blankets are embroidered differently. Around me, older, immaculately groomed men sit and smoke their pipes with quiet approval. No idea who these guys are. Might've seen one or two of 'em and their turbans when I was in the thick of my chercher work, but they all got the look of first-class power brokers. Or warlords. Same thing, really.

The nearest one leans in and says, in a voice that sounds like sand whistling and thunder clapping at the same time, "What are you smoking?"

Which gets everybody—and I mean everybody—in the whole joint on their feet and cheering.

"Lemon-mint." My go-to. The crowd goes nuts again.

The warlords all look on with approval, all these guys looking on who are way above my pay grade, the type of people you hope to never come across in my line of work. They're usually the wealthy bad guy at the top of the conspiracy. Sometimes, they're the answer you don't wanna give to the client who's paid you to find someone impossible to find. And now they're looking at me like I'm some sort of hero. And here I was gettin' on Zoe for being involved in all this politics wahala.

And I think this is it. This is the extent of it. But then the crowd parts and, holding my shisha pipe in one hand and a swinging dish of fresh coals with tongs in another . . . is Zanga.

He's got bandages and a still-purple lump above his left eye, and he stands stock-still at the circle's entrance. Soon as he sees me, doesn't move a muscle.

"You gotta be kiddin' me," I whisper under my breath.

Then Zanga seems to make a decision. He lays the pipe down in front of me in complete silence. Balances the hanging coal dish on his forearm, takes a coal between the tongs, blows out some sparks in a bit of practiced flourish all the guys here know to do, places the coal on top, then does it all again with two more coals. A small hand towel appears out of nowhere, and, with it, he scrubs at the floor area around my feet. This is new. Then he stands, hanging coal dish over one arm, dirty towel folded over the other, nods, and heads back the way he came.

Most shocking thing I've seen this week.

When I finally settle in and start smoking, most folks leave me in peace. Let the hero enjoy his quiet so that he can be well rested for the next myth he needs to make, is what I imagine they're thinking. I'm foolish enough to think this might buy me some goodwill with Zoe, or maybe it's a Moussa thing where I've somehow, in ways I got no way of knowing, gotten in the way and fouled things up.

I'm lost in thought, looking off to my right, and that's how I catch Kadiatou. At a table alone with a mug of what's gotta be kafe cupped in both hands. She starts when she sees me. I've gotten so used to people finding me or waiting for me wherever I end up that it's a pleasant surprise when we just happen to stumble on each other. I go to pick up my shisha pipe, but Zanga appears out of nowhere and, with an agility I had no idea he possessed, sweeps it up and follows me to Kadiatou's table.

Kadiatou watches the whole exchange—me sitting down, Zanga setting down the deluxe shisha pipe gently by our feet, him handing me the mouth end, him asking "Tea?" and me saying "Pot" and Zanga then hurrying off—without a single word.

"Don't know if I'll ever get used to this," I tell her, puffing.

"You'd be surprised," she says back, with an arched eyebrow and a smirk.

"Power corrupts," I joke, and puff. "You gonna tell me what I did to deserve this or just let me live the myth a little longer?"

"You deserve to be the hero for a little bit. Just for a little bit, though. Can't have you getting a big head or anything like that."

"No, we wouldn't want that."

"No, we wouldn't." She giggles. Another life, I'm trying to get her to do that more often.

"They're launching an investigation."

"Who?"

"The Red-and-Blacks."

"What?" Kadiatou's line about being the hero rings differently now. Mention the Red-and-Blacks to anybody old enough and watch their eyes film over. Their heads will fill with visions of arson and looting, of pitched battles that razed whole chunks of the city. Lynchings and executions. The Red-and-Blacks weren't sent to where the fighting was most brutal, they threw themselves at where the fighting was most brutal. They went looking for that. When they couldn't find it, they made their own brutality. That was the counterinsurgency strategy the French turned to when they needed the war to go back their way. Black caps, red tunics, black trousers, red gloves, black boots. They say the gloves on their uniforms started white but within the week were drenched in the blood of their victims. Soaked through so deep no amount of washing could clean them. They started out as the vanguard, then the French army made the sorodassi, figured they could do the rest themselves while not turning the entire population against them. Then when they realized that was a foolish thing to think, the Red-and-Blacks came back. And so did the nightmares. Heroes went to jail when the sorodassi caught them. Heroes went missing when the Red-and-Blacks caught them. I gulp. Loudly. "To investigate the bombing?"

"No." She leans in and actually smiles. "The mass grave."

I drop my shisha pipe.

"There's an investigative unit in the Red-and-Blacks. After the war, the government reformed the unit, because they knew that we dugulenw wouldn't ever agree to be a part of any system that had those genocidaires in it. They're an independent force now, headed by someone back in France. So, no provincial government oversight here. They don't have to answer to anyone here, don't have to bribe anyone here, and they can prosecute and send back to France anyone here. For trial and punishment. At first, this was just going to be a gendarme cleanup operation, then the authorities saw just what was in the debris. Bones. Old bones. Whoever blew up that development knew it was on a mass grave. And they wanted the authorities to see that evidence. Whoever blew up that development knew exactly what they were doing."

She's waiting for me to say something. But I'm not gonna give it to her that easily. When news of the mass grave went out, she probably thought long and hard about everyone she must've told that bit about the mass graves to. Everyone she pointed the developments out to. Because she knows there's no way it was an accident. And targeting a place where there was no chance of civilian casualties ain't exactly the jatigewalekela way.

"Anyway, the official running the investigation is what they call a hard-ass. Only Allah might be able to stop that man from doing his job."

"This is good news, then."

She shrugs. "Depends on who wins the election tomorrow."

"You said this was a done deal."

"He presents his findings. It's up to whoever's in charge to incorporate the evidence into the Commission. If the Commission happens."

Kinda expected it to be too good to be true. Not a win, but an almost-win. In this game, though, an almost-win is dangerously close to a loss. I don't have the heart for politics. There might be something I can do to nudge things further along. Depends on other people doing the right thing, though. I can only do my part and hope and pray. It's weird, feeling like I got a say in my own destiny. Like I can help, in however small a way, to change things. Blowing up that Adam Island development looks like a big thing, but I got perspective now. I know it's part of something larger, something I might not live long enough to see. But something I can work toward anyway. "Hey."

"Yes?"

"The girl. Who started all of this for me. Can you . . . can you tell me about her?"

Kadiatou's face softens. For a long time, she just looks at me. Then she puts her hand on mine. Squeezes, then lets go. "Her name was Hawa. She had a scar on her left knee from a childhood accident, and she always asked for more pepper in her soup. She . . ."

CHAPTER THIRTY-SIX

I'm a bit surprised to find Moussa in his office and not out on the street somewhere being the dugulen-colored face of law and order. But let me accept this gift of serendipity without picking it apart.

He's got a few sheets of parchment in front of him, a stamp pad, an inkwell and a quill sticking out of it. On the two front corners of his desk are small flag displays, a miniature of the French flag and a miniature of the Royal Family's crest. No windows, just a hook on the wall for his long coat and a stack of files on the floor in the back corner. Moments like this you realize that policier with all the sexiness and action of their job are really just civil servants. Didn't know what a civil service was till I joined the sorodassi and suddenly people had to wear a uniform and everyone's offices—those who had offices, at least—all looked the same. It's that sameness. And seeing him like this, it diminishes him. Paperwork. There was never any paperwork in the dugu.

But here I am darkening his doorway with an armful of scrolls. I knock, and he looks up, a note of surprise flashing in his eyes before it's gone. Then his head's back down.

"What do you want?"

Takes me a moment to step in. I keep wanting to remind him that despite all of this, despite everything that's happened, the attacks and the manipulation and the half-lies and the danger we put each other in, he's still my friend. "Can I?"

He gestures to the empty chair in front of him.

I take my seat then motion with the scrolls and he nods silently at his desk, so I set to unrolling. "It's info on the bombing."

And now there's a warning in his look. Something between "you better not be wasting my time" and "how mixed up exactly are you in all this" with hints of "I'm really tired right now, can't you see what I got on my plate" for seasoning.

"Here, just take a look at this." I've marked up all the relevant bits. If the Mize were to ever get these back, I'd be charged enough fees for damaging their documents that I might as well forfeit the clothes on my back and anything I could ever hope to get from chercher work in the future.

"You gonna tell me who was behind it?"

"Come on, Moussa. I'm trying to help."

"Why are you bringing this to me anyway? The Red-and-Blacks are on this. Not my jurisdiction anymore. That ship sailed." And it's your fault, I can tell he wants to tell me.

"I'm sorry, brother." I don't know if I ever told him that, don't know what it's worth. But it feels right to say. He's got his worst-case scenario, and that might not've happened if I hadn't stuck my nose deeper than he'd wanted. Couldn't help myself. And even if he technically got that ball rolling, I'm not innocent in it. "This is info on the property."

He pushes whatever paper he was annotating off to the side and leans over the ledger and the maps.

"See, this here is the building development that got bombed. And see these letters next to it on the map? Well, you got the same letters here, here, here, and here. All housing developments owned and operated by the same guy." I move the ledger to the center and show him the sheets with all the names and the letters and numbers next to them. "And this is the legend. That series of numbers here, that's the building designation. Like a code. This means hospital or medical facility or whatever, this means office building, this means living quarters. Now, those numbers and letters I showed you on the map? Take a look at this guy here." And I jab at the page.

"Honoré Mirbeau de L'Isle-Adam." Moussa looks up at me. "The jagokèla. The businessman."

"All the housing developments are Adam Islands."

"Dumb name for housing developments."

"I mean, it's not that dumb."

"And they're all called that?"

"I don't know, maybe, I only saw the banner on one of them. Anyway, look how far out they are from the rest of the city. Past the Ethnic Quarter, even. Does that make sense?"

"How the hell would I know?"

"Moussa, it doesn't. If you're building housing for pieds-noirs emigrating from France, why would you keep them so far from the heart of the colony? What's out there? There's barely any irrigation, and only one of them is even by a river."

"They're not farmers, Boubacar."

"How do they plan on flushing their toilets?"

Moussa shrugs to concede the point.

"I'm saying each of those spots was chosen for a reason. And that reason has nothing to do with how well those français are gonna be living or not. He didn't pick those spots for the view."

"Then why build there?"

Here it comes. I brace myself. "You know what's there, Moussa."

Moussa is silent staring at the map for a long time, and his face is hard, unreadable. And I know he's got one eye on the past, one eye on the future. He's looking at what was done, sees the doing all over again. And he's playing out the future in his head, thinking through all the different ways this could turn out. Each vision's got more blood in it than the last. If I were a policier, I'd wonder if I should be prepping for more attacks at those sites. More revelations. If I were Moussa, I'd wonder how much longer I got before my neck is in a guillotine. He remembers what the sorodassi did. Amazes me a little that he forgot in the first place. Some people can do a horrible thing and just move on. I wish I weren't so jealous.

"And I bet Honoré Mirbeau de L'Isle-Adam knew that." I lean in. "You wanna buy land, you have to go through a whole process, and yet this guy gets property deeds and building grants just like that." Snap my fingers for added effect.

"Bring this to the Red-and-Blacks. After the election, they'll dig into this. Sorry. Phrasing."

I shuffle some of the papers again and bring out the map. "See this here? This is a warehouse. Out past the French Quarter."

"Yeah?"

"Owned by the same guy."

"So?"

"This was a storage facility for the bombs that got used on the French Quarter."

Moussa's eyes go wide. "What? How do you know that?"

"I got asked to deliver something there. Cart full of something. Well, 'asked' isn't exactly how it got put to me."

"Again. Let the Red-and-Blacks deal with this. Bring it to them after the election."

"De L'Isle-Adam doesn't want the election to happen. He's been trying to disrupt it this whole time. You think he didn't know what his warehouse was being used for?"

Moussa's look is somewhere between a frown and a glare. "Be very careful with what you say next. You're implicating a bossman in a terrorist attack."

I'm doing more than that. I'm implicating a bossman in the serial killing of dugulenw to steal their organs, create bombs, and influence the election. And a terrorist attack. "Look outside, Moussa. The Murutilen's gonna win. He's got every reason to keep that from happening, because if that happens, every housing development gets shut down, nobody moves in, nobody pays him rent. His money's on the line in a big way, brother. We don't know what he's gonna do next. The election's tomorrow. This is his last chance."

"You don't know that the Murutilen's gonna win." He's quiet when he says it. That threatening kind of quiet. "There's more people in the city than just the Ethnic Quarter. City's more than the outer arrondissements."

"But you don't see them, Moussa. You don't hear how they chant his name. Man, walk through the Twentieth and tell me it doesn't just feel different. Different from how it's ever been. People walk different. They're not scared anymore. You saw them that morning at the explosion site. They were ready to throw down with the gendarmes! The gendarmes, Moussa! Before, you couldn't get a dugulen to look an ofisiden ye in the eye, never mind a gendarme. You told someone to get in the slow line at a checkpoint, they started moving before you finished your sentence. Look at them now. Moussa, it's happening."

"You really have changed."

"He's got that effect on people."

"You met him?"

"Yeah. We talked. For a long time."

There's a bunch of stuff happening on Moussa's face that only hints at everything he must be thinking right now, all at once probably. "What are you asking me to do, Bouba?"

"Just . . . just look into it." I get up.

"What about your—"

"Keep them. It's evidence. Maybe it can help point you in the right direction or something."

"Bouba . . ."

"I'm gonna go get you more proof."

CHAPTER THIRTY-SEVEN

Kadiatou's up on the rooftop of her party headquarters.

It's still funny coming up here and not being surrounded by that honor guard. Takes time unlearning how to be someone's prisoner.

"It's quiet," she says when I arrive at her side.

"Never really looked at it from this view. Except, you know, when I was with you." I got my hands in my pockets to keep them warm. Breeze picks up. "You do this often? Look at the city from up here?"

"Sometimes. You can't during the wet season, of course. But . . . during Harmattan season, it's perfect. No matter what's going on down there, up here is peace. You could be watching a riot but from this view, none of it reaches you. None of the sounds, none of the smell. Well, almost none of the smell. Fire burns less hot up here." She takes a deep inhale, then blows it out slowly. "I get it. What the Floaters are after. From all the way up there, what must we all look like? The whole of us? The collective. Can you really see it all from up there? What must that look like?"

"Beautiful," I say. And I can't tell if I mean what she's talking about or her. Either way is the truth. "I'm surprised it's not jumping tonight. No parties?"

"Everyone's getting ready for the big day."

"You nervous?"

She shrugs but doesn't open her mouth to say anything.

I catch her gaze and she's holding back so much anxiousness. She's practically shaking with it. Or maybe it's the cold. I wish I had a blanket for her. "We're almost there."

This time, she smiles right at me. And it's like everything I've gone through to get to this very moment was worth it. "Yeah."

"Hey, come here. You're freezing." And I open an arm for her.

She doesn't even hesitate.

She's so warm against me that I forget where I am. It's soft and gentle and warm. My times with Aissata were never like this. Kadiatou buries her head in my chest and I put a hand to her head.

And slowly, first my feet, then hers, leave the ground.

As soon as her toes dip, she tenses against me. Fear in her eyes when she looks up, a lightning strike of terror, but whatever she sees in my face is enough to calm her. She's still wide-eyed, but she's loosened against me. She lets me hold her.

And we get higher and higher.

She grips me tighter. "How?" But it's not with shock or that angry, loud kind of surprise. It's more wonder. And a little bit of joy underneath. Like seeing a magic trick as a kid, before you learn cynicism and hurt and that most things in the world are fake and that miracles more often than not have an explanation behind them. You're just seeing the impossible thing and you know in your heart it's real. It's just as much a part of your universe as gravity.

"I don't know," I tell her. And it's the truth. I don't know how. I don't know why. But I've always been able to Float. And even when I pretended not to, I knew what it meant. What it connected me to. That night breaking out of Honoré's office, it wasn't the other Floaters who broke my fall. It was me.

It's a mystery to me. How I've been able to do it without having to mutilate myself. It was always something to keep to myself. A secret. Even though I have no idea who I was hiding it from.

We keep going higher and higher until Kadiatou starts shaking against my chest. When I let us both back down, the front of my shirt is wet with her tears.

CHAPTER THIRTY-EIGHT

"How'd you know?"

Honoré Mirbeau de L'Isle-Adam doesn't turn around at the sound of my voice. He doesn't seem the least bit surprised. I can't see his face, so that's only a guess.

I close the window to his study behind me and walk slowly around him and his desk. The whole room's been cleaned up, made to look brand new. But there are still traces of the gun battle that went down the last time I was here. A bit of chipped wood on the vertical of a bookshelf. A burn patch on the ground. The desk is completely new. But it looks exactly like the old one. Maybe he's got a whole warehouse full of 'em. When one breaks or he gets tired of it, out it goes and in comes a new one. All that craft and all that money, all the sweat and resources that went into it, swapped out on a whim. I think I hate him.

When I can see his face, there's a new scar circling his left eye. It makes him look battle-hardened. Makes him look like he's actually done shit other than sit behind a desk his whole adult life.

He stretches out a hand to indicate one of the new, intricately carved wooden chairs in front of him. The cushion is new too. "Or would you prefer the floor like a proper dugulen?"

I take the chair. "We're both in-between men. Why not lean into that?"

He reaches into a desk drawer and pulls out a bottle of dark liquor and two glasses. Then he thinks better, puts the glasses back and pulls out two dishes. In-between men. Pours one for himself and one for me. Then he hands me my dish.

"How'd you know?"

He waves his hand. "Jumping right into it. That's far too gauche. Sit with me for a moment. We've the whole night."

"Don't you got a date for tomorrow? Your guy Savadogo? No campaign dinners for him? No last-minute push?"

Honoré laughs. "Oh, he'll be fine. There comes a point when you've done all it is in your very considerable power to do. You've put everything in place, now you just wait for the weather to change."

"You rich enough to change the seasons too?"

"We are days away from the wet season. One last Harmattan and it'll be over."

"Why'd you call off the assassination attempt?"

He drains his dish, then turns it over in his hand. "In the end, the mogofagala was unnecessary. But I think you knew that. If I'd had you on my team, you might've advised me properly. Better than these sons of goats surrounding me. You might consider it. I pay handsomely. Either way, why create more problems for Savadogo after he wins?"

"He wins, nobody's gonna respect him. They'll figure he cheated."

"Is that my problem?" He pours himself another drink.

"You scared that coming after the Murutilen would expose you? They'd tear you to pieces if anything happened to him."

He laughs, then sips this next drink. Leaves plenty left. "Nobody in the Ethnic Quarter even knows my name."

"And the investigation? The Red-and-Blacks?"

He swats the idea like it's a house fly. "That'll go away too. Savadogo will win. There will be no Commission. The Red-and-Blacks, well, we'll see what they find. Whatever they do bring back to Paris, well, why should Paris care about what happens in some rural colonial backwater?"

"And your properties just keep making money."

"Exactly. Are you sure you don't want to work for me? You're wearing the same thing you wore the last time we saw each other. I can at least promise you a change of clothes."

"How'd you know about the mass graves?"

He sighs, annoyed, and finishes his drink. "You were in the sorodassi."

I sip my drink to keep from answering.

"Did you keep count?"

"Of what?"

"Of how many dugulenw you killed."

I glare at him over the rim of my dish.

"The Red-and-Blacks get all the credit for wartime atrocities, but I knew the second I first saw that haunted look in your eyes that you too had watched dugulenw asphyxiate on their own blood as they bled out beneath you from a balle you had fired. I imagine it was as easy as flipping a switch for you. You already had français in you. In the right light, you look every part the diéman. A simple lie to tell yourself, then you pull the trigger. All in service of an empire. Did you think the empire would reward you? Give you a commendation and some cash to go with it? A trip en première classe to the Fatherland?" He waits for me to respond, to indicate he's gotten to me, but I give him nothing. "You've probably told yourself you don't know why you did it. Why you joined. Why you killed your fellows of the dugu. But I think you know. You wanted to be them. You were closer than the rest of us. Your father made sure of that. And you lied to yourself, told yourself that couldn't possibly be the reason, because you knew how inane and impossible such a wish was. If you had a little of the dugu in you, you had all of the dugu in you.

A fractured self. Irreconciled. So you take it out on your fellows. How did you know I was building on mass graves, hmm?"

"I was told."

Honoré's smirk gets wider. "I think you knew. I think you knew because you . . . cleaned out . . . those duguw. The diéman you served with, where did they all go after the war? Back home across the sea, isn't that right? Did you not think to follow them? Follow your father? You see, when we first met, I had no idea who you were, but I've since learned a great deal about you. And aren't you the most fascinating person I've ever met? What do the policier say? 'A criminal always returns to the scene of the crime,' non?" He puts the dish down. "The landscape was different before the city came to be. I'm sure it must have taken you a moment or two to realize what it was you were looking at. The land binds us, Boubacar. You and me. We are linked by it. Bound to those plots of land by blood. I'm helping you. I'm making sure no one ever has to know what you did."

"There were rebel fighters in those villages. They would have killed innocents to get what they wanted. We were only following orders."

"Oh, I know. They were my orders."

"What?"

"Of course, you wouldn't know. I was so far up the food chain there would be no way of knowing who was directing you where. But I pointed your unit to those villages. You and I both know there were no fighters there."

"You sent us to massacre civilians."

"And you did it. Even after you found no weapons, you lined those dugulenw up against the wall and . . ." He mimes aiming a pistol and firing. "You and ton frère Moussa. All this time, you've been searching for expiation, hoping someone would punish you for your crimes but too afraid to actually give voice to the horrors. Too afraid to do the work. Let me help you. Get out of my way, and let me save you. You and your brother, Moussa."

Footsteps behind me have me on my feet reaching for a weapon I don't have. A weapon I couldn't have brought myself to use anyway. Because right in front of me, a hand cannon aimed right at my chest, is Moussa.

"What the hell are you doing, Moussa? Put the hand cannon down."

His expression is unreadable. "Trailed you here. Watched you walk right up a wall to get here." Then, a sneer. "You're one of them. You're a Floater." His tone when he says it . . . a million beatings from Zanga and his goons couldn't equal that.

"Don't tell me you work for him now." I try to match Moussa's disgust, but there's too much hurt in my voice.

"Civil servants in this country aren't paid nearly what they're worth." This from Honoré.

"It's over, Bouba," Moussa tells me.

And when Honoré gets up from his seat, I believe him.

"Where the hell are you going?" I snarl at Honoré.

"Why, my ship leaves at first light. I will be sending Savadogo my congratulations from the Fatherland." He reaches Moussa. "Please don't make too much of a mess. I just had this room cleaned."

Then I'm forced to watch Honoré walk past toward the door to his study.

"That'll do, de L'Isle-Adam."

At first, nobody but Moussa realizes that those words are meant for Honoré. He makes it all the way to the door before he stops. "What's that?"

"I said, that'll do." Then Moussa turns his back to me and swings his gun arm up at the jagokèla. The bossman. "You're under arrest."

"What are you talking about? Under arrest? Enough with your jokes. I'm leaving."

"For the intentional murder of noncombatants during wartime, for knowingly engaging in financial crimes connected with said murder, for interference in election-related processes, for conspiracy to commit political assassination, and I'm sure if you give me time, I can think up a few more charges."

"Tu n'es pas sérieux!"

Moussa takes two heavy steps toward Honoré. "Speaking French isn't gonna get you out of this."

Honoré growls, "But my security will." He goes to call for his guards, but just then, figures uncurl from the ceiling. Dressed in all black with their faces wrapped, they slowly float down to surround us all, blocking Honoré's path. Moussa doesn't look the least bit surprised to see them.

It was all an act.

"Looks like I got that proof you were talking about, Bouba." The whole time, he doesn't take his eyes, or his gun, off of Honoré. "You're free to go now. Be safe, brother."

CHAPTER THIRTY-NINE

She's out in front of her house like there's nowhere else she could possibly be sitting on a morning like today. She doesn't look at all surprised to see me. There's even another chair at her table. And the pot of tea looks like it's just been boiled.

Her invitation's wordless.

So, I take my seat.

Most of the French Quarter has come down. Français dig through the rubble. In a few places, reconstruction has started. Wooden beams, sheets of scaffolding. Hammers hitting nails. And the quiet hum of conversation while the workers work and the builders build.

She's watching it all happen with an unreadable expression. Sips her tea regally, almost like a machine.

A bunch of diéman walk past, alone or in groups, dressed for the polls. There are a few polling places dotted throughout the destruction. The français make orderly lines. Some of them are solemn. Others are festive. One father has a little boy on his shoulders while his wife casts the family's ballot.

The old lady pours me a cup.

I take it and bring it to my lips.

"Rain's coming."

CHAPTER FORTY

It hurts.

It hurts so much.

The stitching at my stomach has started to come undone just like they said it would if I moved so soon after the operation, but they don't know, none of them do, none of those zealots, what it is to feel regret. Regret that rips the daytime sky in half so that night pours through. Regret so great it opens up the earth and swallows your home and spits it out as a jumbled, blurred mess. That's what my feet shuffle me through. The twisting alleyways where children kick a football with the brown walls as their goalposts, they're empty now, strewn with wooden toys or rotten, spoiled cabbage. The small shack crammed behind market stalls, the shack where dugulenw from the city would come to teach the dugu kids French, it's empty but there's howling coming from inside, the curtained entryway a mouth with beads for teeth, swaying in the night wind, speaking at me in a language I can't understand. I don't know where the Temple is. This place where Bamuso took me after I'd broken my arm. This place where Fa would sit and wait for his physician friend to finish so they could go off and drink palm wine and play mancala. The market is hollow, swimming around me, and howling, and everything hurts. But I can't let them know I've been here.

I bang myself against an abandoned booth, and it's only when I try to right what I've knocked over that I hear their voices. Barking out commands, then someone hushing them, then their voices again, quieter but still insistent, where even their questions sound like answers. Which way did she go. Is she still here. Is someone hiding her.

The shadows. The shadows will hide me. That is what the French-language school is telling me. It is welcoming me. I peel myself forward, lifting my blood from where it has spilled, calling it back to me. The blood framing my footprints, the blood splashed onto the shelf I ran into, the blood running down my leg, I call it all back to me, Float it to me, but I cannot call it past my fingers. I cannot put it back into my wound, my opening. Revenge I can't put back in my body.

The beads stir when I pass through them. I want so badly for them to grow still, for the wind to stop, this same wind that is carrying to me the voices of my pursuers, I want the Harmattan to stop, to bring warmth back to the night, to clear the dust from my lungs. I want the crops back, the rain, the world that the storm hides from me.

But the Harmattan is indiscriminate. It hurts as much as it helps, and when the ofisiden ye and the policier run past, I realize that my footprints are gone. Not just the blood but the impressions my heavy feet left in the dirt.

It hurts so much that I curl into a crescent moon on the floor. I'm running out of time.

I will die on this floor.

The man named Oumar described the home, and when I'm sure the ofisiden ye are gone, I crawl forward. I don't have the strength to Float my blood from the floor.

But when I'm outside again, my city is clearer to me. I know where I am. I'm at the border of the Twentieth. I can see that the centre-ville is not far from here. It feels like a few steps, but it feels like it took me a moon to take them. But then I see it. The mud and stone building, the three floors, the door that surely opens onto the stairs that will take me where I need to go.

The city is empty, but candlelight glows in the homes around me. I peer through a ground-floor window, the scene hazed by drapery. And there's an entire family inside. Two families, maybe as many as three. They are so loud I should have heard them from the other end of the arrondissement. Ba. Fa. Balimamuso. Dogoké. Knémoso. Kanime. All of them and more. Three generations of them laughing and arguing over the food they're eating. There they are. My family. Brought back to life.

My feet leave the ground, slowly. The wind is softer, gentler. It cradles me, leaves me supine so that below my back is an invisible bed of feathers pushing me higher and higher until I can peer sideways into the dinner scene. My tears float in pools by my eyes, rise from my cheeks in small, shimmering bubbles, and I Float slowly, silently, through the window. A breeze ruffling the curtain. The laughter, the spices, they wash me, and I see it. Love. Its chaos, its power. Its effortlessness.

I loved my family.

A young boy, too young to speak, to make more than the simplest of noises, sees me. He is the only one. Only when he looks at me do I notice that some of my blood has freed itself. It floats in stringed beads from my stomach, and I struggle to pull it back but I cannot hold myself up and hold myself together at the same time. Pain. More tears bloom at the corners of my eyes. I will scare this child. He will point his family to me. They will be frightened. They will call the ofisiden ye on me, and I will have failed.

I crane my neck, twist myself, and see a wooden door, and I try to swim to it, hoping it is unlocked, that no one will see me, that no one will hear me fumble at the handle.

The boy stands. He has a fist to his mouth. He has gobbled four of his fingers. Without a word, he waddles through the dinner scene, and everyone is too busy arguing or chatting or joking or laughing to notice the child stand below the window, staring up at me, the child who sees me looking desperately at the door, the child who waddles over to it, raises himself on his toes and nudges the handle with his saliva-covered hand. Then he stands to the side, his face as blank, his eyes as wonder-struck, as they ever were. And I Float, and I tell him thank you with my eyes, and I swim through the air into the darkness of a staircase.

The rectangle of light closes behind me.

I'm so close.

The wind can no longer carry me. I crumple. The mud steps claw into my stomach. But I dig one hand into the wooden paneling and pull and pull and pull.

He's on the top floor. That's what Oumar told me.

So I climb. The blood is on the stairs. I squeeze my eyes shut to call it back to me, to Float it from the dirt and the grooves in the wood, but I cannot finish its course, so it hangs in a thread behind me, what once connected me to my mother's womb, and I take it with me to the top floor.

Now that I am still, I can bring my blood and sweat back, and with my remaining strength I bang on this door, hoping, praying that he is here. For if he is not here, I will die unfinished. I need to see him. I need him to know. I need him . . .

The door caves in, and I fall through. It feels as though it has been so long since I've let myself be seen by another. I'm not ready yet, and I scurry to the far wall, passing through moonlight where I see I've left a trail of darkness, a thread. My blood. And I crouch, I huddle, against the wall, beneath the window, and I am staring at his face.

It's him.

There is so much to say. I've prepared this speech, composed and recomposed it, so many times. But faced with the enormity of him, the weathered, weary enormity of him, the suffering enormity of him, I can't speak. The man who murdered my family stands before me, his face tired and sad, his hands wrinkled, his clothes tattered, and I can't speak. My throat. It is gone. My words. But I have to tell him.

I have to tell him I forgive him. I have to tell him I forgive him for what he did to my ba. For what he did to my fa. For what he did to all of them. He lives above a family that could have been mine. Is this why? To remind himself? To punish himself? But I forgive you, I want to say, and I begin to cry. Sweat plasters my hair over my eyes, but I can still see him. I forgive you. Just as I forgave Oumar. Just as I forgave the others. I forgive you. Please, let me tell you that I forgive you.

It's quiet. The noise of the family, evaporated. Then come voices. Hard voices. Voices that turn questions into answers. The ofisiden ye.

"Hide me" is all I am able to say. "Please."

And he takes me in his arms, this tired and sad and chilled man, and I try to give him my warmth, but it too is gone. It has leaked out of me and lies in a pool under his window.

He brings me to a closet and tries to be delicate when he fits me into it, then he stares into my eyes, and I think he sees it. I'm shivering, suddenly very, very cold, and I've lost control of my body, my sobs come out as whimpers, but I think he sees it. I think he sees that I forgive him. And he closes the doors.

Then their voices fill the room. The ofisiden ye and the policier and the man who butchered my family.

They talk like they fear me, and I know they're talking about the others. The angry ones, the vengeful ones, the righteous ones, the courageous ones. And yet I just want to let it all go.

I want to leave it behind, let the Harmattan wash my history away. If I can't, then someone like him will find another family, the family downstairs, and another one of me will be born, and I cannot let that happen, so I keep as quiet as I can. The man named Boubacar leaves, and the ofisiden ye tear through the room, but something smells horrible to them and they cover their noses and are quick to leave. I look down and my wound has opened. My stomach. My stomach is leaking. It's over.

Dizzy, the world and all its sounds, all its sights slowly fading away, I wait.

But when no one comes back, I nudge the closet doors open. And, without a word, I stagger to the window and climb through. I cannot Float down, only slow my fall. My legs refuse me, so I have to crawl. I don't know why I'm going where I'm going, but I know what's waiting for me there. Pebbles burrow into my legs. My chest. My shirt tears against the dirt. I've lost a sandal. But then the city square lies before me.

There is a grandeur to it that I can't help but admire. It is so big and yet that bigness is all implication. If I am so grand, imagine what surrounds me.

Yes. It is the entire city that surrounds you. The entire city will see me. Will see what I have done.

I pull myself to the very center of the dais, and I come to my knees. The pain has given way to numbness, but it's not a heavy numbness. It's a lightness. And just like that, I'm rising.

The air pulls me by the shoulders, straighter and straighter until my toes no longer touch the ground. I will rise and rise and rise. The Harmattan will not wash me away. It may cover my footprints. It may swallow my house. It may fill my hiding places with sand. But it can no longer touch me. I will be here. I will always be here. I am home.

My city looks so beautiful from this height.

Acknowledgments

My thanks to my editors, Ruoxi and Sanaa, for their work shaping this story and, more importantly, for their enthusiasm. To my agent, Noah Ballard, for steering me through some of the choppiest seas yet. To Mark Smith for a glorious cover and Christine Foltzer for immaculate cover design. To Caro for being my loudest cheerleader not related to me by blood. To my copyeditors for their meticulousness. To C, for everything. And, lastly, to Professor Grimstad for that Detective Fiction class back in '08.

About the Author

Christina Orlando

TOCHI ONYEBUCHI is the author of *Goliath,* a Locus Award and Dragon Award finalist, the young adult novel *Beasts Made of Night,* which won the Ilube Nommo Award for Best Speculative Fiction Novel by an African, its sequel, *Crown of Thunder,* and *War Girls.* His novella *Riot Baby,* a finalist for the Hugo, Nebula, Locus, and NAACP Image Awards, won an Ignyte Award, the New England Book Award for Fiction, and an ALA Alex Award. He holds a BA from Yale, an MFA in screenwriting from the Tisch School of the Arts, a master's degree in droit economique from Sciences Po, and a JD from Columbia Law School.